PHOEBE'S
HERON

PHOEBE'S HERON

Winnie Anderson

CRISPIN BOOKS

Crispin Books is an imprint of Crickhollow Books, an independent press based in Milwaukee, Wisconsin Together, they create books for readers of all ages of lasting quality and positive social impact.

For a complete catalog of all our titles or to place special orders:

www.CrickhollowBooks.com

Phoebe's Heron
© 2018, Winnie Anderson

Crispin Books
ISBN 978-1-883953-91-1

For more, visit the author's website:
www.WinnieAndersonBooks.com

For my mother,
and in memory of my father,
with love.

Hope is the thing with feathers
that perches in the soul.

Emily Dickinson

ONE

I T IS ALMOST NIGHTFALL before I finally see the cabin. The horses snort. Their heads shake and droop with exhaustion. They are on their last tether. That's no wonder. This final leg of our journey has been steep, twisty, and all uphill. A real climb. My nose crinkles at the sweet-sharp smell of horse sweat. Nurse Daisy doesn't like it when I do that: she calls it my "rabbit-twitch," but she isn't looking at me.

We are silent, all of us, father in the front with the driver, and Mother, Daisy, Paulie, asleep in her lap, and me, wide-eyed, wedged in the back seat. The only noise is the rattle-creek of our straining stagecoach, the jingling of leather harnesses, and the horses slow plod. I pull my lap robe tighter around me. The stage, open, has only a flat canopy top for protection, which does nothing to keep out the wind and cold.

A minute later we are at the top. The rough road levels out. A sense of relief at having made it washes over me. Before the driver comes to a complete stop, Father hops down onto the ground. "Quick, Phoebs, I want to show you the cabin's walls," he says. I untangle myself from under the lap robes as fast as I can and jump into his embrace.

I love seeing Father so high-spirited and full of ginger. He's been grim-faced for most of our trip. It's because of Mother. She's sick. That is why we are moving to the mountains. Her doctor says the cold, dry air will heal her lungs.

More than anything else I want Mother to get well. Father, Paulie, and I will do everything and then some to make that happen. And so will Nurse Daisy. I feel a little bad for thinking this so soon, but I miss Denver, my best friend Lisbeth, and the way things were before Mother got sick. All of our lives have been turned upside down since we began planning this move to the mountains.

Trouble is I've come to expect that this overcast sky that is always above us these days will burst open and pour down a needle-hard rain. Nurse Daisy doesn't stand for that way of thinking. She says the sun is stronger than any old buckshot-colored cloud. When its mind is set the sun can burn through even the darkest gloom.

Daisy always adds an exclamation point to her arguments. And by the way, Phoebe, she'll add, since you've lived in Colorado your whole life haven't you figured out that the sun shines here most days.

Yes Daisy, I know that. It's why so many sick people are coming to Colorado. Daisy is smart, never misses a trick. I imagine she will hug me too. It's her way of saying she understands what I mean. Sunny days don't mean much when someone you love is sick.

Father catches me in his strong arms. Paulie is still sleeping in Daisy's lap. How a three-year-old can sleep through the bumpiest bone-rattling stage ride up a mountain is a mystery. Or it's because Daisy's lap is as soft as a pillow. She probably wouldn't like her lap being described in that way, so I'll keep that thought to myself.

Mother is quiet and awake, tired from the journey. Father took care to wrap her with thick lap robes, cushioning her against the lurch and jolt of the ride that the rest of us felt. Not that anyone complained. That is how it should be, Mother's comfort first. He could have put an egg in there with her and I doubt it would've broke.

Father takes the lantern from the stage and carries me to the front door of our newly built cabin. His step is sure-footed. He puts me down. We are standing at 8,100 feet above sea level, he says. The cabin sits on a headland that juts out like the prow of a ship. Steps away from where we are standing are rock cliffs that drop hundreds of feet to the valley below. Even though Father has had a fence built to prevent missteps, being so high and so close to the cliff's edge sets the butterflies in my stomach fluttering.

Supposedly we have a clear view of Columbine Lake from here. Although it is a rare occurrence, according to Father, who has been here many times as the cabin was being built, the clouds have sunk so low that they now fill the valley beneath us. We are on ground that is higher than the clouds.

A dark, snake-like, wavy line in the distance marks foothills behind the lake. Light is fading fast. It is the first time since early this morning that I'm not sitting on something moving, either the train or the horse-drawn stage. With the butterflies in my stomach from being so close to a steep drop-off, and the clouds below me, all of a sudden my legs are wobbling. Father puts a hand on my shoulder to steady me.

"Sea legs, Phoebe. You've got sea legs."

According to the map of the United States hanging in my classroom at school, Colorado is thousands of miles from both the Pacific and Atlantic oceans. I must look puzzled because Father explains. "When a man's been at sea for a long time and then finds himself on land again, the ground, for a while at least, seems to pitch and roll underneath him, like it does for a newcomer on a ship."

He is beaming. Obviously the ground beneath him isn't churning. I want my land legs back.

Father lifts his lantern and pushes it close to the cabin's walls. A moon of golden light illuminates the massive logs. They have a warm reddish tint. "Look," he says, "hand-adzed logs chinked with mud, sand, and the secret ingredient." He looks down at me as if waiting for me to tell him that that is.

I shrug. Absolutely no idea.

"Honey."

"Honey? Why not molasses or maple syrup?" I ask. Mother's relatives from New York always send us Vermont maple syrup each spring.

Father laughs. "Why not indeed. Both would probably work, but don't you think we ought to save the maple syrup for Daisy's flapjacks?"

I nod. He's right about that. Daisy's flapjacks are full moon perfect.

Father runs his hand over the logs. I do too. They are bumpy and yet smooth. "Nary a tendril of wind can get through. As tight as can be," he says.

In the stage Mother coughs. The sound is faint. Most people – had there been any around – wouldn't have heard anything. Or, if they had, they wouldn't have given it a second's thought. To us the cough is as loud as the roar of the train. The lines around Father's cheeks deepen. The corners of his mouth turn down. His good mood is gone as fast as it appeared. Paulie has woken up now too and is beginning to fuss. Father rushes to the stage to help everyone out.

I should follow. At twelve years old I'm expected to help. Instead I stand alone in the thickening twilight. I face the valley and stare into the clouds stirring beneath me. The wind has picked up. Darkness presses down fast and hard in the mountains.

Mother just has to get better. The doctor thinks this is the best place for her. He had better be right.

A lonely sigh of wind blows frigid air into me, as if I were hollow. A wisp of cloud curls itself around me. I close my arms around my chest, but it is too late. The cold has become trapped inside, making me shiver.

PHOEBE GREER
Ridge, Colo

LISBETH BURNS
3 June, 1900

Dear Lisbeth,

I miss you already. It feels like I've been gone for months when it was just yesterday that we were together. I wish I could get excited about being in Ridge. I know that fancy Pinedale resort is close by, walking distance from our cabin even, I'm told, but it seems like we are at the end of the earth.

I understand why Denverites build their summer cabins here. It's so much cooler than hot Denver, but we came because we had to. Mother's doctor, in the same way a prisoner is sent to jail, has sentenced us here.

I'm only going to complain to you, Lisbeth. Daisy and Father wouldn't stand for it. And they'd be right too. Ridge is a town. It isn't a jail.

It is late. I cannot sleep. Today was long, but there were some funny moments. I hope what I'm going to write to you will make you laugh.

We left the fancy halls of Denver's Union Station early this morning on Cannonball. That was the name of our chocolate-colored train. Its gold trim reminded me of the frosting Cook uses on her fancy cakes. The conductor bellowed *All Aboard* so loudly, in my ear practically, that I almost tripped when I stepped onto the footboard.

I caught a glimpse of our reflection in the train's windows as we took our seats. Mother's face was especially pale. Anyone could have seen that she wasn't well, but her sickly pallor deepened the violet color in her eyes and brought out the shine in her honey-gold hair. As you know she's never had a thing for hats.

Even when Mother is so sick she's still beautiful. Next to her I felt my own plainness even more. Daisy braided my hair so tight this morning that even now, so many hours later, my lips are still slightly stretched. My Mona Lisa smile.

Father got our luggage situated. He pointed to where each of us should sit. Paulie was wide-eyed. This was his first train ride. I never saw a three-year-old so well behaved.

Nurse Daisy is as strong and determined as Father. How a war-horse personality can fit into such a compact frame is a wonder. With Father's point of his finger, Daisy gave an order of her own. "Horsefeathers, Mr. Greer! Don't sit the Mrs. in that drafty seat," she said as he was helping Mother get settled. Father is not used to taking orders. He scowled, but he also moved Mother to where Daisy's finger now pointed.

Right before we left Denver, it seemed that Cannonball took in a deep breath, as if he knew we had a long day's travel ahead of us and that we had better brace ourselves for not only the one hour and fifteen minute train ride to the Morrisville depot, but also for the twelve-mile daylong stage ride into Ridge.

The whistle blew shrill and loud. A blast of coal smoke rushed in the open windows. Then hissing and clanking, Cannonball pushed west and rattled out of the station. Lickety-clack. Lickety-clack. In no time I was asleep.

I woke suddenly when a man sitting a few seats of ahead of us began jerking the bell cord and shouting for the train to stop. Possible calamities: maybe the boiler was about the burst? Maybe Cannonball was about to hit a telegraph pole? Derail?

Passengers panicked. In no time there was a slot of screaming and mayhem, a real lollapalooza. It seemed that no one knew what was happening. As the train slowed, but while it was still moving, people started jumping off. Immediately Father was on his feet, telling riders not to jump. He shook his finger at Daisy, which meant that she was to keep us all seated. She obliged. Not one for orders either, she knows when to trust Father.

He had seen early on what all of the commotion was about. The man's wife's hat had blown out the window. He was set on getting it back for her. Father was mad. A hat blown out the window wasn't reason enough for people to jump off a moving train.

I know Lisbeth you might not agree about the lost hat not being an emergency. Perhaps it was custom-made and bought at Maggie's Millinery! Your father may well have sold it to the woman. Still, the only way to exit a train is by stepping on the stool the conductor puts out on the ground and putting your hand on his forearm so that he can help you off. Any other way, unless it's an extreme emergency, which this was not, is dangerous and stupid.

Father's been in the railroad business a long time. He should know.

Father stepped in when a few men, having figured out why the train was stopping, had balled their fists and were shaking them at the bell-cord puller. Had anyone been hurt by the sudden stop, Father might not have intervened and let the husband suffer his fate.

The best part in all of this was that Mother found the whole thing funny. She thought the passengers looked like a herd of leaping cats scrambling every which way when they hit the ground.

When Mother laughs, everything inside of us shifts and

becomes lighter. The gloom inside me brushed off as quickly as a summer afternoon rain shower. I felt the first stirrings of adventure come into me then. Mother took the scarf from around her neck and dangled it out the window. "Time for a new scarf," she whispered to Daisy and me. Then Daisy hung her purse out the window. We hid our giggles, which of course made it all funnier.

"Good thing no one got hurt," Father said, smiling now.

When everyone was back on the train, Cannonball resumed its uphill climb. Lickety-clack became clack, clack, clack. You could hear each wheel's turn. Uphill is uphill, even for an iron horse. By the time Cannonball pulled into Morrisville its shiny pipes had turned dull. Then, letting out one final blow of steam, as though it were its last breath, the train stopped.

First thing I noticed in Morrisville was the air. Father says thin air means it's hard to get a lungfull. Whatever there was of it, though, smelled clean and fresh. This air is what Mother's doctor wants her to breathe. He says it will be good for her appetite.

Mother is too thin. She needs to eat well. The doctor thinks sleep is better in the mountains too. The dry air cuts down on night sweats. He says the beautiful scenery gives a person courage and hope. I hope he's right.

It was not yet 9:00 a.m. by the time we arrived in Morrisville. Waiting for us at the depot was our stage driver. He had a long beard, wore overalls, a wide-brimmed hat turned up, and was chewing on the end of a piece of hay. It bounced around from his lips like a baton a conductor uses to direct an orchestra. Father packed us in the back seat as tight as sardines in a tin and covered us with lap robes. We could hardly move

He was talkative in the beginning. The road snaked alongside Bear Creek, "gin-clear and full of trout," he said. "Starts high in the mountains at the base of 14,000 foot Mt. Veil and tumbles, twists, loops, and roars down the canyon."

We made our way up the windy road along the creek. The massive rock walls on both sides of us made us feel hemmed in. The temperature fell. The wind picked up. Mother coughed more and more as the journey wore on. Doc tells us that as long as she coughs into a handkerchief none of us will get sick.

But she was so worried about her germs spreading that she leaned far out of the stage when she coughed. The wind whipped her hair into a frenzy. Then Father stopped talking. Paulie started fussing. It seems like no matter how pretty the view, how pure the air, or clear the creek, none of those things could stop Mother from coughing.

Our horses plodded on. Wind, when it's funneling

down through a high-walled canyon bores down hard and sharp. It pays no mind to anyone wishing it would stop. If I had believed in our driver's magic piece of hay, I would have snatched it from his mouth and, like a conductor using his baton, directed a complete turnaround so that the wind would have been behind us and pushing us back to Denver.

Indeed, Lisbeth, I'm going to ask Father if I can return to Denver with him and stay with you during the week while he works and then come back with him to Ridge on long weekends.

Right now! Hopefully we can be together soon.

Your best friend,
Phoebe

TWO

EVEN AFTER WRITING LISBETH, I still can't sleep.
Paulie, of course, is having no trouble at that. Our loft
has two beds. There is a big window between them that faces
the back of our property. When we came up to change into
our sleeping clothes I had a quick glimpse of a few monster
boulders – there's one that looks like a pig, curly tail and
all carved into it – and towering pine trees that were scat-
tered everywhere behind the cabin. Standing in front of
the window and peering into the night made me long for
Denver's streetlights. Then there was nothing do but duck
under the covers and let the darkness, in one gulp it seemed,
swallow us up.

Except I'm still awake, so I get up, put Lisbeth's letter in
an envelope, and go down to where Father is sitting in a chair
in front of the blazing fire. His bare feet are on the thick bear

rug in front of the hearth. Paulie kept putting his foot in and out if its mouth when we first arrived. Even though all of us were so tired, it made us laugh.

The fire is hot, the cabin warm. Flames dance. Popping, crackling, and hissing sounds cut into the silence. A wave of sparks lashes against the iron grate in the hearth. One escapes under its bottom and bounces close to the bear rug, but instantly fades from gold to black. Father moves his foot slightly. Outside the wind howls, seeking a nook or cranny through which to slither.

It won't get through.

Mother, Daisy, and Paulie have long gone to bed.

"A letter?" Father asks, holding out his hand.

"For Lisbeth." I give it to him.

Immediately he starts talking. I will have to wait to ask him about returning to Denver with him.

"What do you think Phoebe? Carpenter or poet? Mother thinks Mr. Spencer is more poet than a builder of cabins."

Mr. Spencer is the man father hired to build our cabin, which is so perfectly nestled among the boulders and pines and within earshot of roaring of Bear Creek down the hill.

I have to think about that. I'm tempted to say poet because of the way firelight pours a velvety luster against the log walls, like liquid gold. And because Mother always has good reasons for what she says. Her words carry weight.

Other ladies speak in a too light and airy manner, flitting every which way and, like a moth, never really getting anywhere. Mother says what she means. She chooses words as carefully as a bluebird flies from branch to branch, swift, beautiful, to the point, and deliberate in its course.

Then I think of the tinkling spring that runs next to the cabin, heading down to Bear Creek, which allows us to have running water and a bathroom.

"Magician," I say.

Father laughs. "Ah, a magician. Maybe so." He looks around the room. "By next summer we'll have a phone and electricity. For now we'll make do with candles, oil lamps, and the fire."

He is silent again. The fire sizzles. The flickering light causes the shadows on the walls to dance.

"Many people want Mr. Spencer to build them a summer cabin. He's a busy man, a bit of everything—magician, poet, carpenter. Solid, dependable, and expensive too, but worth every penny. I've hired him to check on you all when I'm working in Denver during the week. He'll come and help Daisy with the harder chores. And Pinedale Resort is only one-half mile farther up Bear Creek Road. Do you remember Pinedale, Phoebe? You were there once as a baby."

Do I need to answer that? What can a baby remember?

"Probably not," Father says, answering his own question.

"Pinedale's owner, Mr. Dale Jasper, is a friend of mine. Told me that if Daisy needs help, he can arrange for one of the cooks to bring meals over to you."

A meal delivered! Whoever heard of such a thing? Sounds like something an author would write into a fantastical novel. I doubt Daisy would stand for that. She already has a well-stocked kitchen and a high-quality cookstove. Father and Daisy will see to it that Mother eats well. As Doc ordered. Mother's health is what matters most. I know what Father is doing though. Trying to make things easy on us. He can afford do this because his job at the railroad company pays so well.

While our cabin feels like it's remote and on top of the world, it's nice to know that we are close to something as civilized as Pinedale. Now I understand how Father found the town of Ridge. My parents went to Pinedale a few times before Mother got sick. They love to dance. Pinedale's ballroom rivals any of those in Denver. It extends way out over a man-made lake. Mother once said, it's like dancing on water.

Deep lines cut across Father's forehead and down both sides of his mouth. He's fallen asleep in his chair. I climb back up to the loft. Mr. Spencer is a poet, I think now. The staircase is made from logs that have been cut in half. You think a log should be round, but Mr. Spencer made them into stairs by cutting out the middle part and making a flat space in them.

Mother loves poetry. She believes poems should surprise, delight, and bring things together in new ways.

Mr. Spencer's log stairs exactly!

I get into bed and snuggle under the soft quilts. The smell of wood and pine are in the air. I hear the trickle-whisper of our baby spring just outside my window on its way down to fearless, big Bear Creek at the bottom of the mountain.

Tree branches scratch against the walls outside. I imagine they are a witch's long fingernails scrabbling along the logs, trying to find a cranny on which to latch. She won't find one. The vaporous clouds, swirling down below in the valley, are from her smoking cauldron. The wind, sounding like a stormy ocean, is trying to carry everything away, but our well-built cabin will remain anchored to the ground.

Strange, I think, being high in the mountains and feeling like I'm lost at sea.

THREE

I N THE MORNING, THE cabin is eerily quiet, cold. The cozy warmth of the fire has long gone out. Still there is the gurgling of our tiny spring outside the window and the muffled roar of Bear Creek below.

I'm not used to this. In Denver, even on the coldest wintry days, I wake in a warm house to the clatter of horse-drawn milk wagons, trolley horns, train whistles, and sometimes, the bellowing of escaped cattle and the shouts of cowboys trying to corral them back into pens. There, I'm part of a loud, bustling city. Here, I hear only the voices of the water and wind.

Father is stirring about downstairs. He's returning to Denver today and will be gone until next weekend. The railroad business has picked up again. Lines are spidering out all over the state and country. Father's job is to raise money for all the new lines being built. He is very good at what he does and explains why we can afford to have such a nice cabin. I hear him talking to Daisy. He's being careful to keep his voice low so as to not wake Paulie and Mother.

He won't leave before saying goodbye. Like him, I'm a light sleeper and early riser. He's coming up the stairs now. The loft's ceiling beams are so low and because he's so tall, he has to shuffle to my bedside on his knees like a scuttling crab. The thought makes me laugh. Paulie turns over but doesn't wake.

Immediately I whisper the question that has been on my mind all night, the one I intended to ask Father last night but never had the chance. I hope I can deliver the letter I wrote to Lisbeth myself.

"Please can I come with you to Denver? Stay with Lisbeth while you work during the days?"

I'm dressed. I went to bed in my clothes last night. Ready to walk out the door with Father. Of only he'll say yes.

Father looks at me with sad eyes. I wish I hadn't asked. I pull up the covers, hoping he hasn't noticed that I'm in my day clothes.

"Phoebs," he says, "I need you here with Mother, Daisy, and Paulie. It's hard enough that I must be away during the week. I hate having to split the family like this. And I know how much you miss Denver and Lisbeth. Do you have time for a story?"

I pull the chain of his pocket watch and check the time, as if I only have a few minutes, and not, as I do, the rest of the summer with nothing to do, except wish I were back in Denver.

"When I was a very young boy," Father begins, a smile in his eyes, "1864 it was, before Colorado was a state, and my parents had only just arrived in Denver, there was a huge flood. It was big and powerful. While not many people died, thousands of animals did. I remember the stench from all the carcass rot. Many people got sick. Then, on top of that, as it can sometimes be with bad things, coming in like waves on a shore, one right after another, there was a grasshopper plague. Many families lost everything. They had come west with big dreams, of gold mostly, and ended up worse off than they were before coming to Denver. So they went back to where they had come from." Father sighs.

"It was a hard time for the city. The railroad business floundered. I remember my father saying that Denver was almost too dead to bury. You couldn't blame those who left, but do you know what they were called?"

I shake my head.

"Go-backers. They were called go-backers. And I vowed then, even as a very young boy, that I'd never be a go-backer of any kind. This is our home now. We'll return to Denver when Mother is well again."

What Father means is that he will not give up on Mother's health, no matter how hard it is for the rest of us. Mother's doctor believes that being in a higher altitude will make her well. So Father is set on it too.

Stop being such a baby I tell myself. What I really want is our life before Mother got sick. That is a fantasy. Time doesn't go that way. Even Miss Ruby, the fortune-teller above Lisbeth's parents' millinery shop, who people claim has a lot of mystical powers, can't turn back time.

Father didn't call me selfish for wanting to leave with him, but he could have. And he'd have been right. He makes a lot of money, but I know how hard he works and how much he worries about all of us. He wipes a tear from my cheek with his handkerchief.

Then he pulls a blank drawing book from his briefcase and hands it to me. My arm comes out from under the covers. My dress has long sleeves. He smiles, pretending not to notice.

"For you Phoebe. I know how much you love to draw. Ridge is so different than Denver. Go see what's out there. There's a trail that starts at the bottom of our road. Locals call it Bearberry Trail. It winds along next to Bear Creek and goes to the lake. It's well-traveled. As long as you are on it you should be safe. Folks are friendly around here."

I open the book and brush my hand over the heavy paper, as if I'm erasing my old life away. My new one is as empty and blank as the pages before me.

He's right about me loving to draw. It has always been my favorite thing to do. I might like to be an artist one day. I haven't done much drawing lately though, because in Denver I'm always with Lisbeth, either at school, at one of our homes, or in Maggie's Millinery parading around in stylish hats and watching who goes in and out of Miss Ruby's.

Maybe I can draw something from nearby that Mother will enjoy. Bring a little of the outdoors inside to her.

Father glances at his watch. "The stage is waiting for me at the bottom of the road, Phoebs."

It's time for him to go. He kisses my forehead, crab-scuttles on his knees to the stairs, goes down, and in no time is out the door and on his way to Denver without me.

PHOEBE GREER

Ridge, Colo

LISBETH BURNS

4 June, 1900

Dear Lisbeth,

By the time you receive this letter you will have figured out that Father said no. Oh Lisbeth, I dare not grumble too much. Mother has it the hardest of all of us. I never hear her complain. Father told me that my place is here now too. While I understand all that in my head, it's just that I thought once Father heard how much I wanted to be back in Denver and....well it's not going to be like that.

As far as I can tell there's no one my age nearby. Daisy says how wonderful it is to be out of the big, dusty cow town. I'm not so sure about that. I miss our brick home with its big green lawn. Father would hate Daisy's description of Denver as a cow town. He's always trying to convince Mother that one day Denver will rival her home, New York Shitty, as he calls it. Yes, really Lisbeth, he says that. Then Mother accuses him of having too much salt on his tongue. I catch a twinkle in her eye though. She's not really mad. She just doesn't want Father to use that language in front of us.

Good Lord Lisbeth, if they only knew how hard we've tried to teach Edgar cuss words. With his cage on top of a pedestal in the middle of Maggie's Millinery, a swearing parrot might do wonders for the buying-of-a-hat experience. Your father wouldn't even need a puller-in to stand outside the front door urging people to come in.

You must keep me posted on the goings on, like who is going into Miss Ruby's. Remember when we used to put on the fanciest feathered hats or aigrette clips and sway our hips and pretend we were on our way to Miss Ruby's to have our fortunes told.

I miss those days so! Never in a million years could I have guessed how fast everything can change. I wonder if Miss Ruby could have told me that Mother was going to get sick and that we'd have to leave Denver so quickly.

I'm afraid. I'm afraid of what happens if Mother doesn't get better. Daisy says the fear that is in all of us is just courage turned inside out. For Mother I'm going to do everything I can to get rid of my fear, like a dog shakes off water, and stop wishing for my old life back.

Father gave me a blank book. I can't wait to start drawing again. I never seem to have the time in Denver. After I help Daisy with the chores I'm going for a walk on Bearberry

Trail along Bear Creek to the lake. I'll send you a picture of something from the wild!

Soon I hope you'll want to come up for a visit. I do so look forward to showing you around.

As ever, your best friend,
Phoebe

FOUR

MOTHER IS RIGHT. IN the morning light, I decide Mr. Spencer is a poet carpenter. It seems as if our cabin has sprung from the ground as naturally as a tree. Stones from the local quarry make up the foundation, fireplace, and chimney. Mr. Spencer didn't cut down the trees near our cabin. One of them is part of the wrap-around porch. He made space for the trunk to go through the roof. And the steps into the cabin are like the stairs to the loft inside, whole logs whose tops have been sliced into flat steps. The cabin belongs here, perched on this very spot, just as much as the trees and boulders. To make it fit so, the work of a poet indeed.

From the front steps of the porch I look into the valley that yesterday was filled with cloud. Today it is clear. Bear Creek twists and loops along the bottom of the canyon into the valley where it empties into Columbine Lake, a giant splotch of bright blue in the distance. Like a saint's golden halo, the sun's rays bristle up from behind the foothills and cast the water's surface into a bed of sparkles.

Closer in, below the cliff and on all sides of our cabin, and mixed in with tall pines and aspen trees, massive boulders are everywhere. Some stand alone. Others are clumped together. Nooks and crannies make pictures in the rock formations. I imagine there must be a lot of stories in those big, old rocks.

Thank goodness Father had Mr. Spencer put up a fence in front of the cabin. The drop-off is steep. It is a long ways down. We couldn't be here without that fence, especially with Paulie. But it's good to be high, where the air is so fresh. Right here standing on our front porch, I feel like I'm at the top of the world. It's just what the doctor ordered for Mother. Sun. Clean air. High ground.

I help Daisy with the chores. Sweep the floor. Clean the kerosene lamps for tonight. Trim their wicks. Take pillows outside and fluff them up. By mid-morning Mother is dozing in her outside chair. Paulie is playing at the woodpile. Daisy gave him the job of bringing in logs for the fire. It will keep him busy all morning.

Daisy is standing at the side of the cabin, hands on hips, one eye on Paulie, the other of a patch of ground she intends to make into a garden. She and Mother have been talking about it endlessly. They want flowers that bloom well into the fall. Roses. Lavender even. They know it's more of a challenge at high altitude than it would be in Denver, but they are determined. Mother calls late blooming gardens filled with perennials "live-forevers."

I put a fried egg leftover from breakfast between two pieces of bread, wrap it in a clean cloth, and tuck it into my lunch pail. There's also room for my drawing book and pencil. I'm going to walk Bearberry Trail to the lake and find something to draw.

The trail follows alongside the creek. It has big wide curves and tight loops. It feels good to be outside walking. I like being alone too, which is a new feeling for me. In Denver all of my time is spent with Lisbeth.

The sun is strong, the sky an intense blue. Not a cloud in sight. Sun diamonds glitter up and down the creek. Water riffles over the shallows, sandy in places, pebbly in others. Huge boulders sit in the creek and alongside its banks. Some are the size of small rooms. Water flows around them and swirls back in a kind of waterfall. In those parts the water is forceful, deep too. A little scary. The sound of rushing water is everywhere, shouting, whispering, always on the move. I suppose it's been flowing like this forever. I feel so small standing next to that creek.

The gentle wind smells of pine. I still cannot get a lung-ful of air. This forces me to slow down. Otherwise I'll get light-headed. Daisy says the altitude affects people in different ways. She promises that in a few days I won't notice it anymore. It's not unpleasant to me, this slight dizziness.

When I get to the lake, I know immediately that this is what I want to draw. A jewel of blue sapphire, points of diamond-reflecting sun glitter loosely here and there in every which way on its rippling surface. A necklace of tall dark pines circles it, and off in the distance, a wavy line of foothills frames the entire scene. It is the same view I see from the cabin, except that now I'm down in it.

I turn away from the lake and look back to the cliff in the distance. At the top is a smudgy dark thumbprint, our cabin. I can just make out the stone chimney. It blends in so well with the landscape that if I didn't know it was there I wouldn't have been able to see it. I must tell Father to bring the binoculars.

I turn back to face the lake. Few people are about. Bearberry Trail continues around the lake but I am content right here. Off to my right is a small cabin with a long dock extending into the water. A fisherman stands on it, his line cast into the lake.

Nearby is a marsh. Black birds with a spit of red on each shoulder sit poised on cattails. The red pulls my eye right to it, like the center of a bull's eye. They sing, "Oh-ka-leee! Oh-ka-leee! Oh-ka-leee!" I sit on a patch of grass and begin to draw. I lose all sense of passing time.

FIVE

A FEW DAYS LATER I'M on Bearberry Trail walking to the lake, not thinking about anything when an animal of some sort barrels out from around a corner and runs straight at me. It may as well be a ghost or the devil himself. My heart, about to burst, pounds against my ribs. I can feel its deep thud, thud, thud.

I know how a cornered mouse must feel as a cat approaches. The poor little thing, frozen with fear, sees the cat's whiskers twitch and smells its rank breath, knowing in the next few seconds he's about to be swallowed up.

Father once said never to run away from a wild animal because that can trigger its instinct to chase prey. There's no chance of that. My feet are rooted to the ground. My brain struggles to catch up. A bear? Mountain lion? What should I do? I can't answer any of these questions because I've turned to stone.

I open my mouth to scream. Then I close it. I must look like a fish.

It's a dog for crummy's sake. A dog whose full-on run into my space has terrified me. I take a quick breath. This is the best I can do, get a half-lungful of air into me.

He is a tall dog, all black except for a white, zig-zag lightning bolt-shaped patch on his chest. Big thundering paws—one white, the rest black—clomp on the trail, sounding more like a horse than a dog. Long legs. Big stride. I feel faint. It has nothing to do with the air being thin. I tell myself to calm down. Take a deep breath. The dog must sense my fear.

"Mike! Mike!" shouts a boy running out from around the same curve, chasing the dog. The boy's head wobbles a little bit from side to side. Mike's ears flop every which way. Both of them are sure-footed and at the same time have a spring in their step. They go together, this boy and his dog.

Mike skids to a stop in front of me, as if uncertain as to how to proceed. He looks back to the boy for guidance. "Stay Mike," is the command.

Now I see that Mike is quite the opposite of an angry bear or mountain lion. He is a friendly, energetic and curious dog, alert and sensitive to his master's every move. Fear drains out of me as fast as air from a popped balloon. I come into my skin again, let out a deep sigh. I put the back of my hand in front of Mike's nose. He sniffs. His nose is cold and wet. I scratch him behind the ears. He nudges his head into me and closes his eyes.

"That's Mike, my dog. He likes ya'. I'm Jed. Ya' new here?"

Jed is a little out of breath too, but unlike Mike, whose tongue is dangling out one side of his mouth, Jed's isn't. He has penny-colored hair and is wearing knee-breeches. His faded green shirt is ragged at the neck; his sleeves, also frayed, are too short.

I think that whatever he is feeling can be read on his face. He's like Mike in this way. Nothing is closed off. Jed is looking at me funny, likely seeing that my clothes are too fancy for just a walk on the trail, and that I'm not from here. Though I've been begging Daisy and Mother for divided pants for days now, I'm still wearing my Denver dresses and petticoats. To him these must look out of place.

"Mike's a friendly dog," he says, looking at my fancy-laced boots.

I nod. In one hand Jed carries a long gun, and in the other a dead bird, a duck. Its feathers: red, green, gold, and blue, still pretty, shimmer in the sunlight. The eyes, though, are glazed over with death.

"'Aven't see ya' before. Ya' new here?" he asks again.

"I'm from Denver."

Jed crinkles his nose the same way I do, the way that bothers Daisy so. I can't see my own nose rabbit twitch – as she calls it, but when I see Jed do it, I don't think it looks all that bad.

"Pa says Denver is all ballyhoo, bustle, and razzmatazz. No tank-ya'," he says. "Why ya' here? Ya' stayin at Pinedale with the rich folk?"

He didn't say 'with the rich folk' in a mean way, like some people do.

"No. My family isn't at Pinedale. My Mother is sick. Her doctor thinks being in the mountains will be good for her lungs. I'm Phoebe." Mother and Father expect me to shake hands and curtsey when I meet someone for the first time, but doing that now just seems odd.

Then Jed surprises me. He puts out his hand. I give him mine. We shake.

"Ah, a 'lunger.' Lots of 'em coming to these parts. Rich ones, that is," he says.

We don't say anything for a while after that. The silence grows between us, but it doesn't feel awkward. Then Jed says, "My Ma died givin' birth to me."

"I'm sorry," I say. Again we are quiet.

I hear the creek rushing, always rushing on, while people are being born, while people are dying. Rushing on since forever it seems like. Mike stands up and goes to lean against Jed's side, as if wanting to take the weight of his master's sadness off of him.

Jed points to a big flat-topped boulder in the creek, close to the bank, water hurrying around it. "Ya' got rocks like that in yur little creeks in Denver?" he asks.

He doesn't give me time to answer.

"Ya' tink ya' kin jump onto it?"

SIX

BEFORE I CAN SAY anything, Jed has put his shotgun and dead bird on the ground, picked up a stick, and taken a mighty leap onto the boulder. "Come Mike," he calls.

Mike doesn't hesitate. He crouches, as though spring-loading himself to harness the power stored deep in his muscles. He jumps onto the rock in a single bound. I didn't know dogs could fly.

Jed reaches his hand out to me. "Come on, Phoebe. I'll help ya'."

Jed's green eyes snap with fun.

The boulder is not far from the bank, but it looks farther away the longer I look at it.

I'm not sure I can make it, but when I look into Jed's eyes, they are saying *you're not in the city, this is what we do here, you can do it!*

I put everything I have into my leap. For the second or two I'm airborne over Bear Creek, I feel like I'm flying. I'm as light as a feather.

When Mother was healthy, she and Father loved to dance. Father used to push all the chairs and sofa in our living room to the walls so he and Mother would have space to dance. My job was to put the phonograph's needle on the thick spinning disc without making the scratching sound that made my goose pimples rise like they do when someone runs their nails across a blackboard. The way Father lifted Mother off her feet and twirled her around made it seem like she was flying too and that she also weighed no more than a feather. He said Mother wasn't a feather, which made everyone laugh, but went on to say it can seem like that because she knows how to move.

When she gets well, Father keeps saying, he'll take her to Pinedale's ballroom and dance all night.

Jed is strong. His hand-grip is sure. The second my hand is in his, I feel safe. If a tornado suddenly comes out of nowhere, Jed will not let go. I'm as sure of that as the sky is blue. He will not let me tumble into the creek. Besides, I'm in a dress. If I topple into the creek, it will be a spectacle.

We are standing on the huge boulder now. A stagecoach can easily fit onto it. It is the size of a small room and flat on top except for one side that gently slopes down to the water. Jed throws a stick for Mike, who gallops down the sloping rock and plunges into the creek, splashing about, trying to snatch the stick in his mouth before the current carries it away. He gets it and brings it back. Jed stands near the boulder's low edge, so Mike doesn't have to jump back onto the rock. He takes the stick from Mike's mouth. After a few more throws Jed hands me the stick. I throw it again and again. Mike it seems can go on at this game for hours.

Eventually Jed and I sit on the rock, warm from the sun. Jed takes his shoes off and dangles his feet in the water. Mike, soaking wet now and likely miffed that the throwing of sticks has stopped, jumps onto the rock with the stick in his mouth. He drops the stick next to Jed. His feet are spread apart, his body and head low, as he winds up for a twist. I know what's coming. Fine water droplets spray off him every which way as he shakes. I see a prism of rainbow colors as the sunlight reflects off this glittering shower in a kind of halo. It is a huge shake. I tilt my face into the falling droplets. The cold water feels good.

Jed throws the stick one last time for Mike. "Okay boy, fetch."

I want to take off my shoes and dangle my feet into the creek like Jed. Instead I put my hands in the water. Ladies don't take off their shoes like that, but I don't think Jed cares a whit about those things. The water stings with cold. I pull my hands from the creek.

"The Bear starts at High Lake at the base of Mt. Veil. Thaws in the spring and is fed with snowmelt. That's why it's so cold. Ends up in the sea somewheres I 'spect," Jed says.

Mike is between us now. "Lie down," orders Jed. He does. We pet him. His dark fur is almost dry. It feels warm. The color black pulls in the sun extra strong. Mike's chocolate eyes never leave Jed. They keep an eye on each other, Jed and Mike. I scratch Mike on his head between his ears. He looks at Jed before resting his head on my lap.

"He's taken' t'ya'," Jed says.

"Maybe, but he's checking with you first, before he does anything."

"We pardners, me and Mike. Good bird dog. Been together a long time, since he's a pup. I trained him. He rustles up birds so's I kin shoot 'em."

"Why?" I ask.

Jed looks at me as if I have three heads and not one of them has any brains.

"For money, of course. Shoot 'em for money. That's how me and Pa live, huntin' birds. We plume hunters. Send their feathers t' Denver. Dealers pay good money for feathers. The prize, the one we's really lookin' for, is the great blue heron. Gray-blue feathers. Them's what me and Pa need to shoot."

"I've seen those hats," I say. I could tell him a lot more; that Lisbeth's father owns Denver's finest millinery shop, Maggies. That I've spent many hours there with Lisbeth in front of the looking glass trying on fancy hats with big feathers and stuffed birds on them.

"Miss Fancy Pants," he teases.

There's nothing mean in the way he says this.

"I'm wearing a dress," I say. For some reason this makes the whole thing funnier. We laugh.

We are standing now on our island of rock, about to jump back onto the bank. Bear Creek ripples over the shallows. It is so clear I can see the colors of the pebbles on its bottom.

Things look different now. For the first time since I've been up here in the mountains, I feel as though I'm on the inside of things, and not, as I have been, looking at this strange outside world as if I were a stranger. Jed's world is coming alive inside of me. I'm not thinking so much anymore about Lisbeth and my old life in Denver.

Jed leaps off the boulder. Mike follows. Jed turns around and extends his hand again. I take a few steps back, gather my dress, and run and jump. When I land half way up the bank and grab onto his hand, he pulls me up the last bit. I feel as though I have just arrived. My two feet, finally, are firmly planted in the here and now.

SEVEN

WHEN I GET BACK to the cabin there is a horse tied at the fence. He rears as I approach. I'm not as afraid as I was when Mike ran at me. The horse is bigger, but he's also tied up. And right from the start, I can recognize a horse for what it is, a horse.

I veer far from his thrashing legs. He's making quite a commotion. A man dashes out from behind the cabin. Paulie is right behind him. "That'll do!" he says to the horse and gentles him with one brushstroke of his hand along the horse's neck. I notice that he looks around for Paulie, making sure that my brother is not within reach of the horse's kicking legs.

"And you must be Phoebe," he says, extending his hand.

"Hello Mr. Spencer," I say, for who else could it be? I shake his hand and curtsey. The curtsey makes me feel like a fool. Somehow all that Denver fluff just doesn't fit up here. He has a friendly, calm manner, but his blue eyes pierce me with the steely look of a gunman taking measure of his target. I doubt he gets rattled often.

Mr. Spencer is tall, broad, and has a bristly, twitchy walrus mustache. It's impossible not to stare at it. He must tend to it with care. Though thick, not one spear is crooked or out of place. It is in direct contrast to the mop of dark, unruly hair on his head.

"Come meet That'll Do," he says.

"That's his name?" I ask, pointing to the horse.

"That it is," he answers, smiling. A twinkle comes through his hard eyes now.

I come around to where Mr. Spencer is standing at That'll Do's head. He pulls two carrots from his pocket and puts one in the center of his open palm. "Here's one for you," he says to That'll Do. "See, Miss Phoebe, how gently he takes it."

He hands me the second carrot. "Here you go. Keep your palm open, firm, and steady, like I did."

That'll Do's mouth nudges in, right to my palm. His lips feel funny on my hand, but it doesn't hurt. I resist the urge to pull my hand away. The carrot is gone in a second. "And there you have it. That'll Do, meet Miss Phoebe Greer. Miss Phoebe, That'll Do."

The way That'll Do looks at me, I think he knows we've been formally introduced.

"How'd he get that name?"

"Before That'll Do was mine, he was thought too high-strung to be of much use. Nobody wanted him. I got him for a song. Worked with him until we became friends. Patience and gentle hands were all it took. People are the reason for a horse's problems, not the other way around. I'll admit that at the beginning I had to say That'll Do a lot."

He laughs. "Now I want to change his name to Just Fine, but that'd probably confuse him, so I won't." When Mr. Spencer laughs he tilts his head to one side.

"Your mother has invited me to supper," he says. "Paulie and I have been working in the ice-house all afternoon. Looks like Miss Daisy'll need help cutting out a garden too. Might have to come back tomorrow instead of in a few days."

Paulie likes Mr. Spencer. He's taken the older man's hand and is trying to pull him back toward the ice-house.

Mr. Spencer just smiles at the three-year-old toddler. "Another day, Paulie. Aren't you hungry? Smell all that fine cookin'?" Mr. Spencer picks up Paulie as though he was a sack of potatoes and sits him on his shoulders. Paulie squeals with delight.

It's wonderful seeing Paulie so happy. Since Mother has been sick, most of our family's attention is on her. Paulie gets left out a lot. I'm old enough to understand what's happening. Paulie is not.

Father and Mr. Spencer have thought of everything, trying to make things easy for Daisy and Mother. From my loft window I can see the ice-house. It's tiny and sits against a small hill, like a thumbprint, a little ways back from the cabin. More like a small cave, really, with thick wood doors as its entrance. Inside are blocks of ice Mr. Spencer cut from Bear Creek last winter. It will keep the meat, eggs, and vegetables cool during the summer.

For supper Daisy makes fried chicken with onions and potatoes, watercress salad, and plum pudding for dessert. I help her get everything on the table.

Daisy is shy around Mr. Spencer. I know Mother has noticed this too. He sure loves her cooking though. Mother and I look at each other, like schoolgirls in on a secret. She has good color. We all love Daisy's cooking. Mother asks for an extra serving of chicken. The doctor wants her to eat well. She is, thankfully. It will help her get strong again.

Afterward, Mr. Spencer brings out his fiddle and plays for us. In Denver, music is a grander affair, dancing parties in elegant homes, and everyone dressed in their finest. If anyone had said to me before this summer that one day I'd be in a cabin in the mountains with no one but Mother, Paulie, Daisy, and a carpenter-poet who also plays the fiddle, and whose music was as good as or even better than anything in Denver, I would not have believed it. I guess there can be slivers of good in hard times.

Mr. Spencer gives Paulie a harmonica. No one minds little Paulie adding his noise to the music. Mother's eyes shine. This mountain medicine seems to be working. While Mr. Spencer plays his fiddle, and with the fire roaring in the hearth, and all of us full from Daisy's cooking, I might as well have just reached into the sky, crazy-mad with glittering white stars, and brought one down in my fist, opened my palm, firm and steady, and let it go in our little cabin. We are spellbound under its magic.

LISBETH BURNS
Denver, Colo

PHOEBE GREER
9 June, 1900

Dear Phoebe,

How awful it must be for you! Only fire for heat. No electricity. No telephone. Gads! Sound perfectly barbaric. How is it that you are surviving?

I'll be frank. I don't understand (my parents don't either) why your father insists that living in the mountains is better for your mother than in one of the sanatoriums in Denver. There are some very nice ones. Certainly your father can afford the best. He is one of the richest men in Denver! And besides how could your parents drag you and Paulie to such an uncivilized place?

I know how much you'd prefer to be in Denver. Just think if your mother were here, then you'd be here too, with your best friend, me. And I don't understand why your father won't let you come and stay with me?

Ha! New York Shitty! I've been working hard, trying

to teach that to Edgar. A real cuss word! No "dagnabbit" for him. I have to wait for a quiet moment in Maggie's. It's nothing I can do in front of customers. Having a parrot in the center of the showroom delights Father. Says its good for business. Puts people in a good mood, which makes them willing to part with their money.

Thankfully Maggie's is always busy. Feathered hats are still very much the rage.

Except that, speaking of New York, Father says that there and in other big cities like Boston and Chicago, women's groups are forming to protest the wearing of plumes on hats. Luckily there's none of that here. Really, if women were not going to wear anything that's been killed, well, they'd be walking around naked.

Bonnie isn't any help at the store. My sister is too busy planning her wedding. She is getting everything she wants, especially a handsome and very rich fiancé. She went up the stairs yesterday to Miss Ruby's.

Father says that having a fortune-teller above Maggie's is as good for business as having a parrot in the middle of the showroom. He gives Miss Ruby hats to wear, hoping the ladies who visit her will want to splurge on a new one for the walk into their sunny futures Miss Ruby has surely predicted for them. I suppose having a busy millinery beneath her business helps Miss Ruby too.

I keep asking if I can have my fortune told. Father keeps saying no. They are too expensive. But apparently not for Bonnie. Miss Ruby told her that she was going to have three children and a very successful husband.

Phoebs dear, I hope you don't have to start school up in the wilds this fall! Do they even have schools up there? If they do, what possibly could you learn from a back-country bumpkin teacher? I wish you nothing but a speedy return to Denver. Your best friend is waiting for you.

Yours truly,
Lisbeth

EIGHT

A FEW DAYS LATER I am sitting, now with my sketch-book, on the same boulder that Jed, Mike, and I sat on the day we met. I'm drawing the elbow curve of the creek and an especially tall pine tree on the bank. The air is clean, sharp, and pine-scented. The boulder is warm from the sun. The sound of rushing water soothes me. Mother is going to get better. I just know it.

I hear barking. "Mike. Mike," I call. He bounds into view. Jed follows. Mike thunders right up to me on the boulder and gives me a slobbery kiss on my ear and cheek.

"Yuck," I say, wiping the side of my head with my fore-arm, not really meaning it. He nudges close to me, his tail wagging. I scratch him on the head between the ears. His eyes half close.

Jed jumps onto the boulder. I'm glad to see them both.

Jed gives one of my braids a playful tug. I refuse to let Daisy braid my hair for me these days, so they are looser and fall apart easily. But at least my face isn't so stretched anymore. Jed has left his game bag and gun on the bank. I can tell there is more than one dead bird in the bag, even though only one long neck is lolling out of it. I don't want to look at that and am glad that he leaves it on the bank.

He's in a good mood.

"D'ya fancy fish for supper?" he asks, hopeful.

"Yes please." I look around for his fishing pole.

Jed catches Mike's eye and points to the bank. Mike doesn't want to go. He looks at me as if hoping I will intervene on his behalf.

"Sorry Mike," I say.

The black dog goes and sits on the bank. Knowing he won't be called back to the boulder for a while he paws forward and sinks down to his belly, his eyes glued to Jed as he rests his muzzle on his forepaws. Mike reminds me of a petulant Paulie, having to do something he doesn't want to do.

I'm wondering how Jed is going to fish without a pole. He points to the gentle sloping overhang of rock that flattens out over the creek. "Under there," he says, "they rest in the rock's shade."

He drops to his knees and then onto his stomach on the flat pancake part of the rock, slowly stretching out his head and shoulders so that they hang off the end of the rock and over the creek. I've seen Maggie, the head designer at Maggie's Millinery, work on a hat with the same careful precision that Jed is putting into getting into the right position on the rock. There is nothing haphazard or rushed about what he is doing. As is the case when Maggie designs hats. They are always beautiful. Expensive too. It's why Maggie has a store named after her. I wonder if the way Jed is planning to catch a fish is as much of an art as designing a hat.

If it were raining and the downward-sloping rock slippery, Jed would have slid head first into the creek. I must have laughed out loud because Jed turns, glares, and puts a finger to his lips, telling me to be quiet.

He spreads his arms wide and brings his elbows back. His hands are in the air, poised, just off the edge of the rock. He is as still as the boulder beneath him.

I hold my breath.

It happens faster than a blink of an eye. His hands slice into the water with hardly a splash. Jed brings up in front of him, as though he were making an offering to a god, a shimmering, foot-long trout!

The fish flaps and squirms so hard that I think Jed is going to drop it back into the creek. In a way, I wish for that to happen. The trout is putting up such a fight. Every color imaginable is in its glistening scales.

Jed does not let it go. He jolts up to a sitting position and bashes the trout's head against the rock. It flaps once and then is still. I look away, but then am drawn back, wanting to see what Jed will do next. Pulling a small knife from his pocket, he deftly cuts off the head and throws it to Mike on the bank. Mike catches it on the fly. It is gone in one gulp.

Jed then scrapes off the silvery scales before slicing the fish open down its middle. He guts it by thumbing up its insides and then grasping the intestines with his fingers and tearing them out. He throws the goop into the creek. It twists like a slow pinwheel in the current. Some of it remains on Jed's fingers. His hands are still glittery with fish scales. He shakes his hands hard and the last bits fly off. Then Jed kneels on the flat slope, reaches down and swishes the trout and his hands in the creek to rinse them out.

He stands, beaming, as he holds the trout in both hands, arms outstretched in front of him. I glance at Mike who is licking his lips. "Stay Mike," Jed says. He's proud of his bare-handed catch, but at the same time he's trying to be nonchalant about the whole thing. He has the goofiest smile I've ever seen. "Pan-sized. For you, Fancy Pants. Take it home and cook it for your Ma for dinner."

I'm touched that he's thinking of Mother now, especially when he's so proud of what he's done. Lisbeth's letter comes to mind. Not once in that letter did she wish for Mother to get better. She wanted Father to put her in a sanatorium in Denver, only because then I would be in Denver too. A selfish streak ran through that letter. Lisbeth swirls through life like a tornado. Everything must revolve around her. I admit, getting swept up in all the bustle and activity is fun, but in front of me now is someone I've known for only a short while who has done something big and is thinking about how that can help someone else.

I give him the cloth that held my sandwich. He wraps the fish in it and then gives it back to me.

"How'd you do that?" I ask.

He looks at the wrapped fish.

I laugh. "Catch the fish I mean."

"Aw, it ain't such a big deal," he says.

It is a big deal, I think, to catch a fish barehanded.

"They rest in the pool of still water under the rock. It's shady under there. They can't see the shadow of hands swoopin' down in on 'em. Catches 'em by surprise. They can't see what's comin'."

"You're quick too," I say.

His smile is as big and bright as the sun.

Later Daisy prepares the trout for Mother's dinner. She dips it in cornmeal and then fries it. Mother insists we all share it, so Daisy cuts it up and gives us each a piece. The flakey white meat is delicious. I tell everyone about Jed and how he caught it.

"So you've met a friend?" Mother asks.

"I have."

NINE

FATHER IS BACK AGAIN for the weekend. Sometimes
I think Mother's health is improving; at other times,
not. There's no telling, at any given time, which way things
are going to go. If Mother is having a good spell, then we are
all in high spirits. If not, we exist under a bleak sky. If she
can't stop coughing, or her fever-chills are bad, and the sun
is shining, everything feels out of balance. Nothing matches
up. It's hard to explain. You think things are going to be a
certain way and then they're not. Daisy calls that "Life."

It's important that Mother be outside, or at least on our
porch, as much as possible. If it's the slightest bit chilly, and
pretty much any wind will make it so in the mountains, even
in July, we pile the lap robes on her, give her a woolen hat for
her head and a hot water bottle to warm her feet. At other
times the fever part of her sickness can make her so hot that

she thrashes everything off before catching the chills again. These hot-cold, cold-hot spells can go on all day.

I don't think Paulie understands that this is not normal. He's pretty much ignored because Mother's health is overwhelming the rest of us. Someone always has an eye out for his safety, but he looks at me every once in awhile as if I have the answers to questions he can't quite form. He needs attention. I give him what I can. It's never enough. He adores Mr. Spencer, who is kindly to him. And of course weekends with Father are special.

Tonight Mr. Spencer is again joining us for dinner. Beforehand, he, Father, and Paulie are outside working on something or other. A pot of stew warms on the stove. I'm setting the table when Mother says, "Mr. Spencer is flustering Daisy. I think it's wonderful."

I nod. Daisy's been cooking all afternoon. I like it when Mother talks about Daisy and Mr. Spencer. It means she's well enough to forget her cough, joint pain, and tiredness. I'm no fool. They'll come back, but at least they are gone for now. I wish I could take a good moment and hold onto it as if it were a rock. I'd never let it go. It seems to me that there's a tinge of sadness to every bright spell because you can't hold onto it forever, except as a memory, which means it has turned into a thing of the past.

WINNIE ANDERSON

The smell of stew is filling up the cabin. "Stop twitching your nose, Phoebs," Daisy orders.

"But it smells so good. I can't help it," I say.

The men and Paulie come in. Daisy gets distracted in the bustle of setting out our supper. I help her put out bowls of mashed potatoes, creamed carrots, boiled turnips, and the stew. We eat. Mr. Spencer keeps telling Daisy she's a good cook. Daisy keeps blushing. Her eyes shine, and she smiles a lot. Mother winks at me. Father is always praising Daisy's cooking, but she never blushes at his complements.

Father hired Daisy right after Paulie was born so that Mother "could get her feet back." Daisy said that I once asked her if that was the trade-off for a baby, a temporary loss of one's feet. I don't remember that. She was probably funning with me.

It didn't take long before Father said, behind her back of course, that she was a war-horse that needed to be in charge of everything. He called her a hot-headed Irish lass too. He didn't think she'd last a month. Then Mother got sick, and Daisy's hot head and war-horseyness began to impress Father more than it annoyed him.

For a while he called her Daisy Do-all and said, this time to her face, she was the best thing that could have ever happened to his family. Daisy said that she wasn't a "thing" and told Father not to call her Daisy Do-all. "Kindling fire" is what Mother calls the two of them, a quick spark and a flash.

But Father apologized about the "thing" thing, and I haven't heard him call her Daisy Do-all again. It seems that for Mother's sake they have arrived at a truce.

Instead Father asked her if it'd be all right if we called her Nurse Daisy, because Mother couldn't be in better hands. Daisy's eyes filled with tears and she said that she'd be honored.

And now with Mr. Spencer's attentions she's like a flower at dusk, coming into its own colors in the fading light, relieved that the harsh mid-day sun has softened. She's looser and more relaxed. She can be very pretty I think, especially when she smiles. Mr. Spencer has brought this out in her.

Father asks Nurse Daisy again if she'd like more help. Pinedale has lots of employees. "And the owner, Mr. Jasper, is my friend. He has offered to send someone to give you a hand," he says.

"Good lordy no, Mr. Greer. We're managing just fine. With Mr. Spencer around and having the groceries delivered from town, I'm getting all the help I need. That'll do for now, sir." Daisy's curls bounce like a schoolgirl's, but when her eyes bore into Father's, he just nods.

"Help is there if you need it, Nurse Daisy. I'll not bring it up again. That'll do for now. I agree."

We all laugh, except for Father, which means he doesn't know the name of Mr. Spencer's horse.

"That'll do," squeals Paulie, clapping his hands. Father glares at him. He doesn't like for his children to sass back.

"Father," I say, "that's the name of Mr. Spencer's ornery horse. That'll do."

"Hey now," says Mr. Spencer with a mock frown as he smooths out his mustache with his napkin, then using his fingers, twists the ends up, head tilting to one side. "That'll do about calling That'll Do ornery."

The meal is delicious. Mother eats everything on her plate. I am full. So is everyone else, but when Daisy brings out blueberry pie and whipped cream, not one of us can turn down dessert.

"We need a name for this cabin," says Father.

"Just Fine," says Paulie.

"That's a good name for my next horse," says Mr. Spencer.

Mother says this will take some thought and suggests we come up with a list from which we'll choose the best one.

"Fox Run," says Daisy.

"High Cliff," says Father.

"Grand View," I say.

"Let's take our time," says Mother. "It's important to get the right one. That'll do for now."

Mother is funny in her own smart way.

Mr. Spencer snorts, which makes us all laugh. "That's the name of my horse, not a cabin," he says.

"How much longer is this joke going to last?" asks Father.

Daisy is laughing so hard that she covers her mouth with the back of her hand and turns beet red. It seems as though none of us, Father included I think, want to leave the That'll Do comments behind.

Until Mr. Spencer starts playing his fiddle that is.

Mother's illness has done this, I think, pared things down to what matters and what doesn't. None of us, I suspect, would have traded in this evening for anything else. My old life in Denver seems so far away now. I doubt Lisbeth will understand when I tell her that I'm glad to be here now.

TEN

I SEE JED MORE AND more in the coming days. Not every day, for he and his Pa are often hunting. Summer is their busiest season. When we do see each other, we pick up right where we left off, as if we are having one long conversation. It's that easy.

I'm usually found drawing on "our" boulder, which we now call "The Rock." He knows he can find me there most days around noon.

"Come on Phoebe," he says today, "I want to show you the pond."

Despite Father's warning not to veer from Bearberry Trail, I don't think twice about going off with Jed. He knows his way around these parts better than I know my way around Denver.

We leave the trail and walk uphill, away from Bear

Creek. We don't say much. Uphill is uphill, but there is an easy silence between us. Jed slows his pace to mine. I'm still wearing my Denver clothes. My dress and petticoat annoy me. I can't move freely. Every once in a while Mike stops and looks back at us as if wondering what in the world is taking us so long. He's panting hard too, even if he's eager to press on. I've never seen such a long tongue on a dog before.

Jed stops at a tree. "Smell it," he instructs.

"Are you trying to make me look featherbrained?"

He laughs. "No ma'am. G'head. Smell it. Ya'll like it," he says, pressing his nose to the tree's trunk. "All Ponderosa Pines smell like this." He takes a giant sniff, "Mmmmm."

I lean in. He's right. It smells sweet, and it reminds me of something. At first I can't place it, but then it comes to me. Vanilla, and maybe with a hint of butterscotch to it too.

For a moment I'm in our home in Denver. Mother is baking a cake and just at the point of adding Burnett's Vanilla to the batter. Jed could not have known that the smell would trigger such a vivid memory. Tears well up in my eyes, blurring everything. I feel one slide down my cheek. I don't want Jed to see this. I wipe my face with my sleeve. Smell a tree and come to tears. What's Jed to think?

He doesn't ask me what's wrong. "Reminds ya' of some-tin'."

It's a statement.

I nod. I'm not going to say anything, but when he looks at me like he understands perfectly, the words tumble out. "Mother and I used to bake cakes. She always added three extra pinches of vanilla – one for me, one for Paulie, one for Father. 'Brings out the razzle-dazz' she used to say."

"And I bet those were the best tasting cakes in Denver," he says gently, not smiling. He must sense how sad those what-used-to-be thoughts make me feel. My guess is that he can see into my sadness because he too has had a big share of it.

We climb on. My legs are getting wobbly. I feel the burn in my muscles, but I'm managing to keep up. The ground flattens out. We turn in the middle of a grove of aspen trees. We might as well have made a sharp right turn in the center of the ocean, but Jed isn't lost. He knows exactly where he's going.

Down we go. The slope is steep. Down is as difficult as up, but we are covering more ground faster, and I'm not so out of breath. Mike disappears, his tail flickering between the trees. I'm almost flying. My feet feel as though they are hardly touching the ground. "Slow down," Jed says. "Keep that up and ya' gonna catapult yourself into somersaults. That'll hurt. Lots of trees and boulders be in ya' way."

A dot of blue ahead. Splash! Mike is already there. He must have grown wings.

"My secret pond," Jed announces. "Not many people know about it."

Much smaller than Columbine Lake, it's fed from a trickling stream of mountain run-off. At the other end is a beaver dam that stems the flow of the stream, keeping the pond full. Water that trickles past the dam flows down past our cabin and then on into Bear Creek.

"Pa says that one day he's gonna shoot them beavers. Pond won't be much if he does. Don't think there's a lot of money for their pelts. I fish here sometimes. With a pole," he adds, smiling.

The sun is as bright as ever. The air feels alive. It shimmers, making the edges of things, trees and rocks, even Jed and Mike, more defined. We sit on a downed thick log and throw a stick for Mike. The pond is deep. Mike is a strong swimmer. His head and shoulders remain above the water and dry while he swims.

"Watch this," Jed says.

Before I can say "watch what?" Jed is up and running to the other side of the pond. He is not one for sitting still for long.

Directly across from where I'm sitting is a steep bank. Jed scrambles up it, his shoes slipping out from beneath him, dirt erupting into a cloud of dust at his feet. He manages to stay upright. Speed helps. He's done this before I think.

Hanging from a thick pine branch that extends out over the pond is a rope with a stick tied to the end of it. Jed takes a thin, long stick from the ground and knocks the rope back so that the branch swings to within his reach. He grasps it with one hand. Then he climbs higher still up the bank. It is slower going now. If he loses his footing he'll have to drop the branch.

Careful now to position both hands on the branch, one on either side of the rope, Jed belts a mighty wild Indian holler and pushes off the bank. "Woo-hoo!" he screams as he flies out over the pond, swinging back and forth, up and down.

I have to do that.

By the time I get to the bank on the other side of the pond and start my climb up, Jed has let go of the branch and is struggling up alongside me. We are kicking up a lot of dirt. "Ya' sure bout this?" he asks.

The climb is steeper than it looks.

I nod.

"If ya' let go, the pond's ice-cold."

"Not going to let go," I croak. I have no breath.

Jed holds the branch, steadying it as I position my hands on either side of the rope's knot.

"Now," I say, pushing off with my feet. Jed gives me a gentle shove from behind.

I soar over the pond, higher and higher into the vast blueness. I wonder if the sky is made of glass and if it will shatter into millions of glittery sharp stars, or will it be soft and cocoon me into its folds, like a pillow.

I'm flying backward. Now swinging forward again, then back. Up and down. Just as Jed did. I could do this forever. My skirt and petticoat fill with air when I go forward and then deflate on the way back. I like the flowy-ness of them around my legs in the wind.

It's not a gradual tiring, but sudden. I'm afraid I'm going to let go.

"Jed," I say.

He must have heard me because I feel his arms around the bottoms of my legs and then around my waist. "Let go, Phoebe, now," he says quickly.

I do. He catches me.

Triumphant! I feel triumphant.

Jed tweaks my braid. "Ya' did it!"

I'm shaky all over. My legs are like noodles. I make my way back to the log on the other side of the pond.

Jed's going to take a few more turns.

"Okay, Phoebe, last one!" he shouts from high up on the hill as he takes off his shirt while holding onto the branch, awkwardly, one arm at a time.

Of course I know what he's planning to do. Mid-flight,

when he's at the highest point, just before beginning the swing back, Jed lets go of the branch, calls "Mike," and splashes down into the pond.

"Like ice!" he sputters when his head comes up from under the water. I hear him gasp for air. Then he's laughing. Mike is swimming to him.

Jed grabs hold of Mike's back and lets the dog pull him to my side of the pond. I think Mike is smiling as much as Jed.

It is the most fun I've had in a long time. Even though Jed has done this before, many times with Mike, this afternoon, I feel, is different for him for him too. Different because he's shared his secret pond, a gift, with me.

ELEVEN

W E ARE ON OUR way back to Bearberry Trail when Jed stops at another tree. Is he going to tell me to smell it again? Given that the last tree made me cry, why he would do that?

He peers closely at the bark. Then he touches it with his fingers. "Scratch marks from a cat," he says.

"A cat?"

Immediately I think of Mrs. Marshmelly, Lisbeth's white ball of snuggles that drives Mrs. Burns crazy because of the scratch marks and hairs shed on their living room furniture. Jed looks at me with his now familiar expression, the face that says I have no idea of what he's talking about.

"Not a fluffy city cat or alley tom, Phoebe. A mountain lion. A real cat. A very big real cat."

He points. "Looka here," he says, "ya' kin see the fur."

With his forefinger and thumb, and with the delicate precision of tweezers, he pinches a tuft of honey-colored fur from the bark. He gives it to me. It feels coarse, like sand.

"All cats are alike ya' know. Ya've seen house cats scratch low on the furniture and then stand tall and do it again higher up. When they do this they have a kind of backward arch in their spine.

I nod. I've seen Mrs. Marshmelly do that many times. She usually doesn't get very far on the higher scratch because by that time Mrs. Burns is yelling and shooing her away.

"It's the same thing here." Jed stands. He's looking for another set of marks. "There they are," he says. "See 'em?"

"Yes. How do you know all this?" I ask.

"Dunno," he answers. "Some things Pa tells me. Some I jus' figur' out me'self. How'd ya' know all the things ya' know bout livin' in the city? Ya' jus do. Live somewheres long enough, I spose, and it gets inside ya'. Be the same if ya' were showin' me round Denver."

Jed's lips curl downward in such a sour vinegar face while he twitches his nose at the word "Denver" that it makes me laugh.

"Denver's not so bad," I say.

"No tank ya', but Pa and me need the city. Need the dealers who pay us for feathers. As long as them fancy ladies want feathers on their hats, Pa and me can make a livin'."

Maybe Jed is right. I can no more see him in Denver than I can see a mountain lion snuggled up on Lisbeth's living room couch.

I remember also in Lisbeth's last letter to me that she wrote of women in other cities like Boston, New York, and Chicago who are protesting the wearing of plumes. Milliners in those cities must be scared that they'll go out of business. Since Lisbeth's parents own a millinery shop, I'm sure the Burns don't want any protest of that sort in Denver.

Jed and his Pa wouldn't want it either. They work hard to get the feathers and probably do not make a lot of money.

I keep these thoughts to myself. Lucky for the both of my friends, those protests haven't yet arrived in Denver. For now, indeed, Denver's milliners, thanks to plume hunters like Jed and his Pa, seem to be doing a brisk business.

PHOEBE GREER
Ridge, Colo

LISBETH BURNS
21 June, 1900

Dear Lisbeth,

Thank you for your last letter. I never knew getting married could be so, well, complicated. Bonnie is lucky to have a sister like you. Good thing people set dates for a wedding. Without one, I suppose, the planning could go on forever.

Things are better here since I last wrote, not nearly as barbaric as you may think. I've met a friend, Jed. He's a plume hunter. I've never given the feathers on a woman's hat much thought before. I'm sure you have, of course. I always knew that Maggie needs feathers to design hats, but I never paid much attention to where those came from.

It all starts I know now with people like Jed and his Pa. Shooting birds is their business. And they need the dealers that pay them money for feathers. It's how they make a living. Lisbeth, have you actually ever met a plume hunter?

Jed's dog is named Mike. They are always together. Mike

is every bit a bird-hunter, as much as Jed and his Pa. Jed and Mike are showing me around Ridge.

The other day we saw a herd of elk cross Bear Creek. One, a six-pronger (we counted), stopped in the middle to take a drink. Jed said that the way his ears were cocked, he knew we were watching him. Mike wanted to chase the herd, but Jed kept him at his side with hardly more than a whisper. During rutting (see the new language I'm learning), which is in the fall, elk can turn on you and charge. Most of the time though they just ignore you.

Jed said that had his Pa been with us, he would have taken a shot at the elk. Frankly if I had been on my own, that kind of thing wouldn't have ever occurred to me in a million years. I forget that my friend and his father are hunters. Jed says that his father doesn't overkill. There doesn't seem to be anything bloodthirsty in how he talks about what they do.

Sometimes our conversations about hunting go in circles. I'm still sorting out the difference between good hunters who like animals and kill them and the bloodthirsty ones who don't like animals and kill them too. Living in the mountains and having a friend like Jed gives me all sorts of new things to think about. I like it.

Don't drown in the wedding plans Lisbeth. If you feel like you are going under, take a quick glance at the blue sky and take a deep breath. Know that I'm probably doing the same thing too. It's beautiful, the Colorado sky. One glance can make you feel new and hopeful again.

Yours,
Phoebe

TWELVE

J ED LOVES TREES. TODAY he tells me to rub my hands
on the white-trunked Aspen tree's bark and then on my
face. "Ya' won't sunburn this way," he says.

I do it.

He laughs.

"You do it too," I say, a little too primly I must admit.

He does. Now I know why he's laughing so hard. He
looks ridiculous with white smears on his face. We look like
half-ghosts, but the white powder from the bark is cool and
soothing against my skin. Lisbeth would have never done
this, I think, not in a million years.

Aspens are my favorite trees. Their heart-shaped leaves
twirl on their stems in the wind, like they are dancing. Jed
says this trembling-quaking way they move reminded the

Indians of the way their women-folk spoke, with babbling tongues. It must have been an insult.

I love the way they quiver. Rather than babbling tongues, each quaking leaf, sensitive to the slightest breeze, is dancing and laughing to its own beat, joyous under a deep blue sky and the sun's dappled rays.

Jed and I cross the creek on the big rocks. A fallen log serves as our final bridge to the bank on the opposite side. It's big, so there's no real danger of falling off. We climb up to the road.

To the left the road leads back up to our cabin and just beyond that to Pinedale. I've never been to Pinedale or met Mr. Jasper. I know that Pinedale is close to our cabin, but it's just past our turn-off and farther than I've gone in that direction. I've heard so much about the resort and Mr. Jasper that I want to see it for myself.

Jed leads me to a small trail that parallels the road.

"I can't imagine Pinedale is all that exciting to see," Jed says. "We'll have to cut across some ranch land," he adds.

I get the sense Jed isn't wild about taking me to Pinedale, but he's already way ahead of me. I run to catch up.

We come to a fence, easy to scramble through underneath. I hear cows mooing. We start to cross a flat, grassy, open meadow. It's not far to the fence on the other side. The wide expanse of grass makes me want to run. "Can you cart-wheel?" I ask Jed.

"Not good," he answers.

Jed is too serious this morning. I'm going to show him my specialty, cartwheels. And right then and there, one after another, across the meadow I go. I'm wearing a petti-coat underneath a long skirt, but I'm too fast for anything to be exposed for long when I'm upside down. I'm on my fifth cartwheel (my record is ten) when I hear Jed shouting at me.

"A bull, Phoebe!"

I stop cartwheeling and try to plant my feet firmly on the ground, which is spinning underneath me. It doesn't feel flat, and my legs wobble, as if they've lost the bones in them.

"A bull! Run. To the fence. Now!"

I look to where Jed is pointing. All of a sudden things get serious.

Huge wide horns. Snorting, pawing. A monster crea-ture, that bull who is about to charge. Me!

"The red, Phoebe. The red under your skirt is making him mad."

I understand. My petticoat is apple red. As I cartwheeled the whirling red must have infuriated the bull. I wonder if I should try to slip it off, but there is no time. I run.

As fast as I've ever run before.

I feel like I'm moving in slow motion.

"Hurry Phoebs!" Jed shouts. "Faster!"

I don't have far to go. I swear, for just a second, I feel as if the bull's hot breath is all over me. I slide feet-first under the fence. My boots rip through my skirt. But I don't care that Daisy will be mad that I've ruined it. Not at all. I can't wait to get rid of the blasted thing.

Jed is pulling me now under the fence by my ankles. It hurts, but I don't fight him. He's strong. For a second I think the bull is going to charge right through the fence, but he gallops up to it at full speed and then stops suddenly in a flurry of dust, bellowing and snorting fiercely.

On the safe side of the fence now, I turn around and see the beast's nostrils quivering fast, in and out. He is giving me the evil eye. I shiver. Goose pimples pop up all over my arms.

"Let's go," shouts Jed. We run to put more distance between the angry bull and us. When we are out of the bull's sight and among the thick pines again, we stop, gasping for breath.

Then Jed laughs as though that was the funniest thing he's ever seen.

I'm not so sure. It irks me that he finds my near brush with death so funny. But here's what I also notice. It's impossible to stay mad at Jed for long. His laugh is starting to make me laugh. That's what I get for trying to show off my cartwheels. Who would have thought, a red petticoat causing such a ruffle.

"The petticoat matador!" Jed calls me.

My face pretends not to find that funny, but it is funny. I can't do it and laugh harder.

I hear the tinkling of bells. Jed tells me we are near the bell man's home. Winston James is his name. He's been collecting bells since he was a boy. He has hundreds of bells, perhaps thousands. Many are kept outside. Those must be the ones we hear. Every year on the Fourth of July he has a bell-ringing party. Jed and his Pa went last year.

We stop and listen. I've never known the sound of tinkling bells to sound so beautiful. Perhaps it's because we are outside and the sun is shining. The jingling of the bells is mixing with nature's own music, the rustling aspen leaves and purling creek.

"Come on, Jed. Let's go," I say. I've heard about Pinedale so much from my parents, I'm anxious to finally see it. Even though it's so close to our cabin, I'm always headed the other way, toward the lake on Bearberry Trail.

"Come on," I say again. I think the bells' sound is magic, but Jed is acting like he doesn't hear them. His usual energy all of a sudden has popped like air out of a balloon.

Most of the time he's yelling for me to catch up. Now it's the other way. The closer we get to Pinedale, the more Jed dawdles. He reminds me of Paulie scuffing the toes of his shoes on the ground when he doesn't want to go somewhere.

We must be getting close. I can see across the main road to the turn-off that leads up to our cabin. Pinedale can't be far now.

THIRTEEN

IT IS ONLY WHEN the smell of freshly baked cookies reaches us that Jed picks up his pace. The trail has
climbed uphill, and we stop at a break in the trees and look
down. Below us we have a good view of Pinedale Resort.

The main lodge is big and constructed with logs. Bear
Creek roars along next to it. In front of the lodge's main
entrance is a big pond. People are fishing there. A group of
riders are heading out for an afternoon trail ride.

Next to the lodge lined up along the creek are cabins that
people can rent for the summer. I know about those. Mr.
Jasper wanted my parents to rent a cabin, but Father wanted
his own place. So he bought the land and hired Mr. Spencer
to build our cabin.

I look up and across the way to the cliff top where I can
see the smudge of logs that is the side of our lake-facing cabin.

Jed's energy has returned. He commands Mike to sit and then stay. "Hurry up, Phoebe," he says.

We head down to the space between the main lodge and the line of cabins on the creek. It feels to me that Jed is being stealthy. He has chosen to sneak in the back way instead of entering through the front. He stops at the corner of the lodge and peers around. He looks back at me and puts a finger to his lips.

I look around the corner too. There is a nice grassy area next to the creek. Two ladies are sitting on lounge chairs there. One has a book in her lap; the other's head is tilted in such a way that I think she must be dozing. Between these two ladies is a table on which there is a plate of cookies and a pitcher of lemonade.

It is quiet but for the roar of the creak, which is why it will be easy for Jed to do what I know is coming. I remain at the corner of the lodge and watch him run to the table and take a quick swipe at the cookie plate. The ladies don't stir. In no time he's back with me, proudly waving his fistful of cookies.

This isn't how I wanted to see Pinedale. I feel like a thief. We are sprinting back up to the trail to the cover of trees when we run right into a very well-dressed gentleman. Quite literally. Jed bounces off the man's stomach and almost loses his footing.

"What have we here?" the man says. I know how bad this looks. Jed and I make an odd pair. We both have white smeared on our faces, and although my clothes are of the highest quality, they are torn and mud-stained.

Add to that the cookies in Jed's hand.

The man is looking at me hard. "And who might you be?" he asks.

"Phoebe Greer, sir," I answer.

His eyebrows rise. "Robert your father?"

I nod. I have a sinking suspicion of who this man is. Father has many friends. I've met a lot of them, and frankly they all look alike to me. Mostly it's in the way they dress, fancy suits and all. I've heard Father speak of Mr. Jasper many times, especially since coming to Ridge. But this, I'm sure, is the first time we've met face-to-face.

"Well then, Phoebe Greer, it's nice to meet you. I'm Mr. Jasper." He puts out his hand.

He has the smile of a Cheshire cat, a big wide one that does not extend to his eyes. A cigar is plugged into the corner of his mouth. I shake his hand and curtsey. This is one of those times I know I have to curtsey. I look him straight in the eye as my parents have taught me to do.

"And how is your mother?" he asks.

"Fine, sir, thank you. I mean, sometimes she's fine, other times not so much."

"Does she know where you are? Whom you're with?"

His tone, particularly on the second question had a sour edge. Mr. Jasper is looking at Jed now, and not in a nice way.

"No," I answer.

Jed hasn't said a word. I know he's hungry and just wants to eat the cookies. He's looking down at his shoes, which I see are full of holes. Is Mr. Jasper going to demand that Jed give back the cookies?

He doesn't. Instead he just says, "Get and don't let me see the likes of you here ever again. You hear, boy?"

If I hadn't been there, Jed's bawling-out might have been much worse. I'm proud that my friend is standing tall and meeting Mr. Jasper's gaze. "Take them, sir," he says, handing the cookies to Mr. Jasper.

Then he runs off into the trees.

"Now, Miss Greer, what in the dickens are you doing running around with a boy like that for?"

"He's my friend, sir."

"Hmmm," he responds, throwing the cookies into a nearby trashcan, as if Jed's hold on them somehow made them untouchable.

He proceeds to walk me home. It's not far, but once we get onto our road, the climb is steep. I don't think he realized how taxing it would be to get me home. He's breathing hard and has a red face by the time we get to our cabin. I am reminded of the sweet-sharp smell of horse sweat, which isn't nearly as bad compared to the rank, worse than bull breath smelling Mr. Jasper. My nose is twitching up a storm. I want to take my fingers and pinch my nostrils, but since we are so close to the top of the road, I hold back. Father and Mother have taught me not to be rude, but this sure is a test. To Mr. Jasper's credit, though, he hasn't uttered one complaint. Maybe that's because he can't. There doesn't seem to be any air left in his lungs.

As soon as I see Daisy coming out to greet us, I say, "Thank you, sir," and dash into the cabin as fast as I can.

I'm sure Mr. Jasper gives Daisy an earful. What Jed did was wrong, stealing cookies like that, but Mr. Jasper has judged him too harshly and too fast. To him, it was obvious that Jed didn't belong at a place like Pinedale and, therefore, needed to be given the boot.

It's true that Jed looks like he doesn't come from money. But that's a mean way of thinking.

Had the cookies been in my hand, Mr. Jasper likely would have taken me into the resort's kitchen and offered me a seat and something to drink, maybe would have placed in front of me a plate of more cookies, warm and fresh, straight from the oven. "If you wanted cookies, young lady, all you needed to do was ask," is what he'd have said to me.

I'm sorry Jed gave the cookies back. He would have enjoyed them.

They looked delicious.

FOURTEEN

THE NEXT DAY DAISY gives me a divided skirt. Finally! No more long skirts or petticoats. Daisy must have been fed up with all the rips, tears, and mud stains on my nice clothes. Scrambling under fences, swinging out over a pond hanging from a branch, jumping onto rocks in the creek, hiking up mountains, and of course, fleeing a charging bull (which I never told anyone about), those sorts of things will wear out city clothes fast. I'd known that for a while, but now Daisy does too.

"These are better," says Daisy. I couldn't agree more, but I tried not to show the huge smile I was feeling inside. A divided skirt with bloomers underneath will make a world of difference. It's as close to a pair of pants I'm going to get, at least for now. What I really want, though, is a pair of blue jeans.

I tell Daisy that I'm going to sit quietly on a rock and draw. Her look says I don't believe you, but she doesn't make anything of it. She hands me my lunch pail. Inside are two sandwiches.

"In case you are extra hungry," she says, adding, "and there's a treat at the bottom."

Mother and Daisy know that Jed is my friend.

Jed and Mike are already on our rock by the time I arrive. I'm expecting him to say something about the cookie incident at Pinedale, but he doesn't. So I don't either.

When I give him a sandwich he looks at me kind of hard. He knows I know he's hungry a lot. A part of him doesn't want to take the sandwich. The other part wants to. "Half is for Mike," I say.

He takes the sandwich, unties the twine from the cloth, and gives half to Mike. It's gone in an instant. Jed eats his half almost as fast.

"Thanks," he says.

And now the air between us is clear. Somehow in that exchange we've settled the Pinedale incident. It is behind us now.

I pull Daisy's treat from the pail. It is a double-sized slice of sweet blueberry buckle. We eat it, every last crumb.

I begin to draw. Jed sits quietly behind me. I've been working on a picture of the big question mark-shaped curve in the creek. Our rock is the dot at its bottom. It's going to be hard to get everything right: from the wavy line of the creek to the gentle way the water widens in the shallows to how in the deeper parts, as it flows around a boulder, it gushes back in on itself in deep roiling eddies.

I want to draw the aliveness of it all. The pines' wind-swept branches. The fast-moving high white-cloud puffs. The buttercups, larkspurs, columbines, and Indian paint-brush, all slightly droopy now from the blaze of the midday sun.

Jed can't sit still for long. He's jumped off our rock and is collecting small stones from the edge of the creek. He comes back, unfolds the sandwich cloth, and dumps a pile of flat rocks onto the pancake part of the rock. "Gonna teach you how to skip a stone," he says. "Nuttin' more than a flick of the wrist. Like this."

I can't see what he did with his wrist. It was too subtle, but the stone flies out of his hand and bounces in a straight line about five times in the creek. I take a break from drawing to stand up and stretch. Then I take the stone Jed places in my hand. I give it a try, a few times. But when I try to throw like he did, my pebbles fly in different directions all over the place, or just plunk straight down into the water. Mike chases the ones that land on the bank. Jed gives up on me pretty fast. I don't mind. He seems happy to have the pile all to himself.

I go back to drawing. He continues to skips rocks. Then he nudges my knee with his foot. I look up. Jed points to a black fox running on the trail. Mike is up on all fours now. Jed puts a staying hand on his neck.

I've never seen a black fox. I thought all foxes were red. The ends of his fur are silvery, as if he's run through a ten-second blizzard and hasn't yet shaken off the light dusting of snow. The tip of his tail, swishing like the end of a paintbrush in a cup of water, is snowflake-white.

The fox slows to a walk, turns off the trail, and goes uphill. He does this elegant prance-walk by curling up one front paw and then leaps into his next step. "There's sometin' he wants, and it's close," says Jed. "Probably a mouse," he adds.

The fox is gone now, disappeared into the pines.

"Draw him, Phoebe. Ya' can draw anything."

That's a compliment. Before, when Jed has looked at my drawings, he sometimes traces along my lines with his finger. He's a watcher, always examining things close up, interested in each and every detail. That is his way.

As I'm turning to a blank page, Jed puts his hand in the book when he sees the picture of a robin that I've drawn.

"Ever hear the story of how the robin got his red breast?" he asks.

"No." Drawing the fox, I guess, will have to wait.

"Ya' see the Injuns had a fire and they had to go huntin'. One small boy wasn't allowed to go 'cause he needed to watch the fire and keep it goin' so it'd still be there when the hunters got back. He was told it was an important job.

"After the hunters left, the boy watched the fire for a while. Then he fell asleep. Soon the fire was jest 'bout out.

"But a robin saw what was happ'ning and flew down so he could fan the fire with his wings, keeping it goin' so the boy could sleep. He did this for such a long time that his breast became very hot.

"And turned red."

I must have a skeptical look on my face because he says, "Really, Phoebe. That's how it happened."

He's kidding me. I can tell. His freckles start smooshing together and his nose is crinkling because he's doing his trying-not-to-smile smile but doing it anyway.

"Do you have stories like that for every animal and bird?" I remember how many times he's talked about a big bird called a blue heron. I ask, "like for the great blue heron?"

He sighs, losing his sort-of smile. Each freckle now stands on its own.

"Pa and me need to find one of those. Has a long neck.

Yellow bill. Blue-gray body. A white head. Black feathers on the side and down his back."

He scrunches up his face again, tightens his lips. He's seeing the great blue in his mind.

"Walks funny, like he's stubbed his toes. Likes to be in the creek, searching for fish. He's awkward, too, when he starts to fly. 'Cause he's heavy and slow. His long legs makes it hard for him to get off the ground."

Jed has a faraway look now, like he is tracking a bird flapping great blue-gray wings, struggling to rise from the water.

"That's when I'll take my shot, when he's strugglin' to get airborne. A great blue, that's like a pot o' gold at the end of a rainbow. Feather dealers pay good for a blue's feathers." He pauses. "But they're hard to find."

Jed's not telling me a story anymore. It's in the tone of his voice. This is very real to him, his need to find this bird. Everyone knows pots of gold at the end of rainbows are not everyday events.

I wonder how many hats and aigrettes I've tried on that have had great blue heron feathers on them. I've never given the feather part much thought. All Lisbeth and I have cared about is how grand we look wearing the hat or clip, as we parade in front of Maggie's Millinery's big looking glass.

We played dress-up. But now, on a rock in Bear Creek, sitting next to me is a plume hunter desperate for the money he gets for shooting birds and selling their feathers. For him it's not a game.

"Sounds like a beautiful bird," I say.

Jed gives me one of those looks again, the one that makes me wonder if he thinks I'm crazy. He doesn't care about a bird's beauty. Birds are his business.

"Phoebs, if ya' see one, ya'd better tell me. Usually they don't stray far from their nests."

"You mean you'd kill the adult birds, even if they had a nest with chicks in it?" I already know his answer. I shouldn't have asked.

"'Course."

The corners of Jed's mouth curl down now, as if he's frustrated at having to explain something so obvious to him, something he thinks I should have known too.

"Gotta go," he says. "Come on, Mike." They leave.

I want to ask him if he wishes he didn't have to shoot birds, but maybe it's better that he's gone and I can't.

I mean, how can he tell a story about a robin being a boy's friend, and then minutes later tell me how he'd take a shot at a great blue heron struggling to fly out of the creek? Because it is not a bird to him. To Jed a great blue heron is a pot of gold.

I guess the difference is also that one is a story and the other is not. Shooting birds for money is something over which he has no choice. What he wishes for or not doesn't matter.

FIFTEEN

I REMAIN ON THE BOULDER long after Jed and Mike leave. I lean back on the warm rock, my hands clasped behind my head, looking up at the big blueness above me. Not one cloud is in sight. I'm waiting for a bird to fly overhead, wings spread, soaring high above me.

I must have dozed off for a while because when I wake up, the sun has dipped behind the mountains. Dusk. I better get back before Daisy and Mother start to worry.

I like this time, not day, not night. A between-time. The sun's light has softened to a violet-silvery hue. The air has thickened. It hangs suspended, paused somehow. Perhaps I'm sensitive to time, in the same way I notice every little change to the light. I'm in a place as ancient and unchanged as the rock I'm sitting on. I am both old and young at once.

I'm a star at the earth's beginning. I'm the last human on earth in an unknown future. I am twelve years old.

I could stay this way forever, caught in this magical slip of time that is alive with joy and which I can't explain. I want to put what I'm feeling now into one of my drawings. I don't think that will be easy.

A squawk pulls me back into the twilight. I peer into the fading light and see him, a mere stone's throw away.

A bird, a magnificent, tall bird stands in the shallows, balancing on delicate, slightly crimson-colored legs, like a dancer. How long has he been there? I wonder.

Long-snaked neck. Gray-blue feathers ruffling in the breeze. White head. Distinguished black plumes above the eyes that extend down the back of his head in wisps.

Step. Pause. Step. He lifts one foot out of the rippling water and places it gently in front of him, then the other foot. He must be foraging for food.

Then he stands motionless, waiting. What does he see? Can he pick out the colors in the stones at the bottom of the creek through the flow of water? A fish's approach? The wing beat of a moth? Or a hummingbird? Me?

Suddenly his head jerks up and for a brief second or two he stares not at me but into me, as if he must make sense of the one thing that doesn't belong. His head bobs and tilts at odd angles. Puffing out his long plumes, he wraps his wings around himself, as though putting on a winter's coat. He coils his neck into an S-shape before lengthening it out. Pointing his sharp yellow bill toward the sky, he croaks out another high-pitched whistle, a harsh sound in the velvety twilight.

My heart jumps a wild beat!

I'm as still as a stone. The great blue heron belongs to this fleeting moment in the same way a rainbow appears in the overlap between the last sprinklings of an afternoon rain and the sun coming out again. I want to claim the great blue and the rainbow as mine.

I cannot. No one can. It's impossible, for they are not for the taking.

Not in any hurry now, the great blue heron softly tiptoes his way out of my view into the question mark-shaped curve of the creek and is gone from my sight.

SIXTEEN

JULY FOURTH! INDEPENDENCE DAY.

Father is here for the holiday! All of us, Daisy too, have been invited to Winston James's place. That's the bell man's home. He's hosting his annual bell-ringing celebration. Everyone who lives in Ridge is invited.

Jed and I heard some of these bells on that memorable day of the bull charge and cookie incident. I remember Jed telling me that he went last year to the party. I hope he'll be there today.

Mr. Spencer will pick us up in his stage. Mother's feeling a bit off today and will stay at home. Daisy says that she'll stay back with Mother. Mother will have none of that. She encourages Daisy go to the party. I know that Mother likes being alone.

Daisy shakes her head. She is loyal to Mother and stubborn. "An ornery mix," Father once said.

Father insists that Daisy go. She turns on him, hands on hips, as if how dare he order her around like that.

"Go, Daisy," says Mother softly. "I'll be fine. Just planning to sit in the sun chair and read."

"Hmmmph," says Daisy, and then adds, "I'd better change into nicer clothes."

Mother gives me a conspiratorial wink. It is only for Mr. Spencer that Daisy will change her clothes. Only he can make her blush and inspire her to want to look her best.

The sun is blazing, the sky an intense blue. It's pleasantly hot. By walking down our road to Bear Creek Road where Mr. Spencer is waiting with his wagon, we spare That'll Do from having to make the steep climb to our cabin.

Bear Creek Road is full of stages and hay wagons and walkers going to the party. Every once in a while an automobile will toot its horn, and the throng on the road splits to let it pass through. Everyone waves. Some have small American flags in their hands. The holiday makes people feel festive. That'll Do has jingly bells and red, white, and blue ribbons tied into the leather straps of his bridle.

Mr. Spencer turns left, off the road onto a bridge over Bear Creek. I know where I am. Not far away is a herd of cows, and a bull who isn't fond of the color red.

Mr. Spencer is talking. "Winston James has this bell ringing event. It's a Ridge tradition, every Fourth of July." He's speaking to all of us, I think, but he's only looking at Daisy. I can't wait to tell Mother that Daisy is all goo-goo eyes for Mr. Spencer.

I see Jed and his Pa. This is the first time I've seen Jed's Pa. He has a beard and, like Jed, is tall, stalk-thin, and wears scruffy clothes. Some tall people don't fit into their height. Maybe they are uncomfortable with standing out in that way, but not Jed's Pa. Daisy would say "a tall glass of water, that one" and mean it as a compliment. Jed's Pa is shaking hands with some of the men and tipping his hat to the ladies.

There is a mix of people here today. There are those like Jed and his Pa, locals, and then those like us, people who, in ordinary circumstances, live in Denver and summer in Ridge. I half expect some Indians to show up. I think they'd be welcomed if they did.

In Denver at my parents' parties all the people are alike. The atmosphere is stuffy. It's too full of curtseys, overdone manners, and boring conversations. Until the dancing starts, I hate those parties. Here, everyone is invited, so there's no hoity-toity guest list. And the mood is lively.

We gather in a small grove, where bells are everywhere. Some hang from thick branches in trees, others are enclosed in brick campaniles. It feels like being in an outdoor church.

Mr. James, a shriveled old man in his 80s, used to be in show business, Mr. Spencer told us, or told Daisy and we overheard. The old man moves through the circles of people crowded into his grove with the authority of a ringmaster from the circus.

This is his big day.

He gathers all the kids and tells us to sit down on the grass. Paulie climbs into my lap. Jed sits next to us. Jed and I are the oldest "kids" in the group. I only sat down for Paulie. Jed sat down for me. I like that.

He leans over and whispers, "Did this last year. I know the bells we want. Ya' Ma come?"

"No," I whisper back. His face darkens.

I see Father talking to Mr. Jasper in the crowd of adults assembled in a horseshoe shape behind us kids. He has an ugly cigar in his hand. He's likely telling Father about the type of company I keep. Both men are frowning. Jed looks at where I'm staring. He shrugs his shoulders, as if there's nothing to be done about any of that now. He's right.

I wave to Mr. Jasper but don't wait to see if he waves back, which makes Jed snort in a sort of muffled laugh. He covers his mouth with the back of his hand. I'm sure Jed doesn't like Mr. Jasper, but he's not holding onto a grudge either.

"Bell ringing," Mr. James is saying, "is a Fourth of July tradition, a celebration of the Signing of the Declaration of

Independence and in honor of the ringing of the Liberty Bell in 1776. To ring a bell today is to remember the courageous individuals who fought and brought this nation into being and those who protect and defend our liberties today." Paulie starts to fidget. Jed settles him by pulling two small feathers from his pocket. He gives one to Paulie. They sword-battle with them.

Mr. James makes a sweeping gesture with his arms to encompass all the bells in his grove. "Bells have called people to work and prayer for thousands of years. They sing in times of joy, and cry with us in sorrow. They send messages. They signal alarm.

"Each one has a story," he says. Mr. James speaks of bells as though they are friends, the same way Mother talks about books.

"Okay everyone. Time to choose your bell," Mr. James says. Jed has been waiting for this. Everyone scatters, and fast. Mother would have said like leaping cats, using the same phrase as when she described the passengers jumping off the train and running off in every which way.

Choosing a bell is serious business. Those who've done this before know exactly the bell they want. There are bells from tugboats, riverboats, school bells, locomotives, and even a few from prisons: old and new ones that range in size from less than a quarter-inch in diameter – set on a table for the youngest bell ringers – to those that weigh a hundred pounds or more and will need two or more men to pull the rope attached to its clapper.

Father picks an old school bell that is big and heavy, but manageable enough for him to ring by himself. Mr. Spencer follows Daisy while she looks for a bell and then suggests an old ship's bell that will be too much for him to ring alone and would Daisy please help him? Blushing, she says yes.

Jed calls me from a stone campanile in which there are three bells, one high up and two below, triangular shaped. He's holding all three ropes, saving two of the bells for Paulie and me. He got there fast. Those are the ones he wanted. He gives me the rope tied to the highest bell.

Mr. James raises one hand, as though he were about to start a race. It's important not to start before he gives the signal. A few people, those on the smaller bells, have to hold onto their clappers lest the wind knock them against the bell before Mr. James lowers his hand.

There is only the sound of the rustling aspen and rushing creek. No one talks. Suspense builds. I hold my breath.

His hand slices down through the air. The ringing begins at one. Thundering. Booming. Tinkling. Singing. Cling-clanging. I keep an eye on Paulie, thinking that all this noise might be too much for him. Paulie is watching Jed, who is giving my little brother such an encouraging smile that if

Paulie had any fear of the loud noise it has evaporated before it ever had a chance to take hold.

The ringing goes out into the mountains and echoes back in deep reverberations. I'm sure Mother can hear this. It seems like a good time for a prayer for her health. I glance at Father, ringing his sizable bell. He is working hard to call out the bell's deep powerful clangs. His eyes are already shut. I close mine.

We ring bells for a full three minutes. That is a long time if the clapper is heavy. My arms get tired.

Jed takes my rope for the last 15 seconds or so. He bounces up and down between the high and low rope. Paulie laughs and is giving Jed his rope when Mr. James gives the signal to stop. I doubt Jed could have managed three ropes, but he would have tried. I'm pretty sure of that.

For a while the air is filled with the presence of bells, even though the ringing has ceased. Then it is silent again, but a sense of fulfillment and a relief at the job well done makes everyone's hearts swell with pride at being a ringer in Mr. James' grove of bells. In addition to whatever personal prayers have been offered, the entire event feels like a collective tribute to our country has also been delivered, the proper respect paid to our country's celebration of independence.

And it's not over!

"Come on, Phoebe and Paulie," Jed says. "Hurry up!"

SEVENTEEN

WE GATHER AGAIN, "YOUNGINS" on the ground, adults standing behind, but this time we are near the entrance into Mr. James's home. There, next to the stairs, on a specially made stand, hangs a big, round, golden temple gong from Hong Kong. It looks like an over-oversized flapjack.

Mr. James points to the two large dragons etched into its surface. They stand on hind legs and with their front claws are reaching out for the world – a big circle –suspended between them. There are oriental characters on the gong too, but Mr. James's memory isn't what it used to be, so we "youngins" are free to come up with what they mean for ourselves, he says. One of them, he knows for sure, is "wishing every one of us a long life."

"There are two ways to ring a gong," he says. First he circles the far outside edges with his mallet, tapping it quickly and lightly. The sound is hardly noticeable, but then it builds toward a crescendo as he moves the mallet quicker and brings it in toward the center with smaller and smaller circles, in the curly way of a looping pig's tail. I imagine crashing waves along a shoreline and the sound gets to where I don't think it can get any louder.

It's a little much for Paulie, who covers his ears and climbs into Jed's lap. Jed covers Paulie's hands with his, and this calms my brother.

Then Mr. James says we are going to ring the gong in a more traditional way. He asks for a volunteer. All hands go up, but Mr. James picks Jed, who takes Paulie with him to the gong. Jed takes the mallet, kneels down so Paulie can easily put his hand on top of Jed's and, as Mr. James instructs, bangs the mallet in the gong's center. This is the sound I've heard before.

Boom! Boom! Boom! Paulie and Jed could do this forever.

Jed gives Paulie the mallet and to everyone's delight he takes a few swings on his own. People clap.

There is a picnic afterward. Mr. James's daughters quickly set up tables during the gong ringing. Jed and his Pa are invited to sit at Mr. James's table. Paulie wants to go with Jed, but Father doesn't allow this. Paulie cries when Father, apparently unmoved by Jed's kindness toward my brother, takes his son by the hand and leads him to a different table.

There are plates of fried chicken, biscuits, potato salad, and pies of every kind. By the time Mr. James's daughters bring out trays of watermelon slices, people are mingling among the bells. Paulie has found Jed again.

Father doesn't stand for this for very long. Careful to not be rude in public – even though I see it as plain as day – Father tells me to go and get Paulie.

"I'm sorry," I say to Jed when I take Paulie by the hand.

Jed waves it off as though it doesn't matter. "People like your Pa and Mr. Jasper don't like people like me," he says.

It does matter. It matters to me, and deep down, I think it matters to Jed. "I'm sorry," I say again.

We are the first to leave. Father and I are quiet on the ride home. Daisy and Mr. Spencer talk and talk. Their chatter sounds as good as the tinkling bells in the wind. I don't think they've noticed the tension that has sprung up between Father and me.

Later I tell Mother everything. I describe how considerate Jed was toward Paulie and how sour-faced Father was toward Jed.

There isn't much Mother can say. "He'll come around," she says. "A lot of Fathers are like that when it comes to their daughters. No one will ever be good enough for you."

Maybe, but that doesn't excuse rudeness, I am about to say. Complaining about Father to Mother isn't going to help Mother get well, so I change my mind and stay silent on the matter. Right now her health is more important than anything else.

Father knows that Jed is my friend. He will just have to live with that. I will not choose my friends based on where they live, what they do, or how much money they have or do not have. Bigger than all those things is what's in a person's heart, how they treat other people.

It seems that Father is a bit short-sighted when it comes to Jed.

EIGHTEEN

AFTER DINNER FATHER HAS a surprise. Mr. Jasper has invited Mother, Father, Paulie, and me to the fireworks at Pinedale tonight. He asked Father at the bell ringing. I suspect he told him a few other things as well.

The best part about all of this is that Mother wants to go. She's tired of people fussing over her and has rested all day. Father promises her a dance in Pinedale's famous ballroom that extends from the main lodge out over the pond. "It'll be like dancing on water," he says.

We haven't been out as a family in a long time. We walk down the hill slowly. Father doesn't want Mother to tire herself out. It's a short walk to Pinedale from the bottom of our road. Mr. Jasper will send us home on a stage. Uphill would be too much for Mother. She's thin. Her dress is baggy, but she is still beautiful, and would be so even if she were dressed in a flour sack.

My parents are holding hands. This fills me with hope.

We cross the bridge over Bear Creek. Approaching Pinedale this way, from the front, is not the way Jed and I took before. I glance up into the pine-studded slope, where, from the small trail hidden there, Jed and I peered through the trees at the ladies sitting by the creek, a plate of cookies between them.

Guests at Pinedale are dressed up. We are wearing our best as well. I'm in my favorite blue dress, annoying tiny buttons and all. My hem is below my knees but, thankfully, it is not as low as Mother's. Otherwise I'd be tripping all over it. Unlike the bell-ringing party to which everyone was invited, locals and summer residents alike, this evening's festivities are solely for the well-heeled guests of Pinedale. And Mr. Jasper's specially invited friends, like us. It is obvious that Jed and his Pa will not be present.

Suddenly hands cover my eyes. "Guess who?"

I'd know that voice anywhere.

"Lisbeth. What a surprise!" I say, taking her hands from my face and turning around to greet her.

She's smiling. It's good to see her too. "I told your father not to tell you," she says, bouncing up and down with excitement. "I wanted it to be a surprise. And the trip was not terrible. Your cabin must not be as far out in the barbaric wilds as I thought."

I point at the high cliff across the road where our rooftop is just barely visible.

"Come on," she says. "I want to show you our rooms. We're staying here at the lodge, of course." She takes my hand and begins pulling me.

Mother nods, urging me on. "We'll have Paulie with us. Meet us at the bridge after the fireworks. Have fun," she says.

It feels wonderful to be whisked away by Lisbeth. On the way to the rooms we stop and say hello to her family in the dining room. They are just finishing their dinner.

"Trout doused in lemon butter and herbs, in case you are wondering," Lisbeth says. "Never had better."

I have, but I don't say anything about the trout Jed caught with his hands. It may not have been cooked as fancy as it is here, but it was a gift, both in the catching and the eating, which makes it the best ever. I doubt Lisbeth would understand that way of thinking.

The dining room has three big stone fireplaces. Even though it is July, all are roaring, taking the evening chill out. At the same time, big screened windows are left open. A thick pine scent is in the air. Each table has a vase of columbines on it.

Lisbeth knows everybody. People always want to talk

to her. I've described her like a tornado because it seems as though everything must revolve around her. But when I'm carried along in her whirlwinds, even if they are all about Lisbeth, it feels exhilarating. Life is never dull when I'm with her.

She insists on wearing a sunbonnet in order to protect her china doll's skin from freckling. Her blond hair is naturally curly. Lisbeth loves to flounce her curls. I doubt she has ever met a looking glass she didn't like. Her blue eyes sparkle.

She gets away with a lot. Daisy calls Lisbeth "a live wire," especially since I told her about Lisbeth trying to teach Edgar, the caged parrot in the middle of Maggie's showroom, swear words.

As if reading my mind, "New York Shitty. Almost there," Lisbeth says as we approach the table where her family is sitting. I laugh so hard I almost trip over my feet.

Lisbeth's sister, Bonnie, looks all grown up. I guess that's what happens to someone about to be married. She holds out her hand, showing me her ring. A stunner, but at the moment I'm more interested in the plate of chocolate-chip cookies in the center of the table. Mr. Burns passes the plate to us. We take one.

"Come on, Phoebs. Let's go upstairs," Lisbeth says.

As we are leaving the dining room, we come fact to face with none other than Mr. Jasper.

"Hello, girls," he says. "Phoebe Greer, how lovely to see you again."

He bows.

I should extend my hand and curtsey, but I don't do either of those things. "You've got your color back I see," he adds.

His thumbs are tucked into his watch pocket. He's rolling back and forth from his heels to his toes. I think he's deciding on whether or not he wants to make me squirm, to embarrass me in front of Lisbeth. After all, the last time I was at Pinedale I had white aspen tree bark smeared on my face and was with my friend who had stolen cookies in his hand.

Mr. Jasper still has a bit of his Cheshire Cat smile along with a gooey wet cigar stuck in the corner of his lips.

Lisbeth has no idea what he is talking about. Luckily she doesn't seem to care. It doesn't involve her.

"At this time of day sir, there's no danger of getting sunburned," I say.

Mr. Jasper laughs. "Well I'm glad you've found a friend like Lisbeth. Take as many cookies as you like," he says, looking at the cookie in my hand.

I want to ask him why he told Father about Jed stealing the cookies at the bell ringing. I can't say for sure that he did, except why else would Father have been so rude to Jed?

I lose my nerve. Mother is so excited to be here. For her sake, I'll not sass back. I'll mind my manners.

"Thank you," I say. For good measure, I throw in a quick curtsey.

"Go on, girls. Once it gets dark we'll have the fireworks. Glad to see your mother doing better, Miss Greer."

"Thank you," I say again, and this time I mean it.

NINETEEN

LISBETH TAKES MY WRIST and we are off. The Burns' suite is airy and spacious. Lisbeth and Bonnie are sharing a room. The beds are covered with handmade quilts that have pictures of bears and pine trees designed in them. Through the open windows it's easy to hear Bear Creek.

No wonder Pinedale is such a popular place.

Bonnie dashes in to change into a different dress for the fireworks. She is not as vivacious as Lisbeth. Probably wouldn't find teaching a parrot to swear funny.

Picking the right dress is serious business for her. Four are spread out on her bed. It appears that Lisbeth and I are on hand for the sole purpose of helping Bonnie with this task. I suppose we are lucky in that the choice is down to four. There's enough luggage in the room for two weeks, but Lisbeth says they'll only be here a few days.

I haven't thought this much about clothes in a long time, either mine or someone else's. Even though I'm in a dress now, since coming to Ridge, I've come to prefer a divided skirt and a good pair of ground grippers. Those make it easier to scramble onto boulders in the creek, swing from a rope over a pond, and hike up and down hills with Jed.

I appreciate Father wanting his own place and not settling us at Pinedale for the summer. Having our own cabin makes us more a part of Ridge than we would be if we were here. As much as I'm enjoying Pinedale, it seems that guests have just packed up their fancy clothes and parties and moved them to the lodge.

I suppose for many people, that is enough.

I've met people like Mr. Spencer, the bell man, and Jed. I think of all the things we've done, including being charged by a bull. My world has gotten bigger for the people I've met in Ridge, those I likely would not have met if we were long-term guests here.

Bonnie is asking me about a dress.

"I like the blue one," I say. Blue is my favorite color.

"Me too," says Lisbeth.

It didn't take as long as I thought it would. Bonnie puts it on and twirls in front of the looking glass, satisfied.

"Phoebe," she calls, "over there on the shelf, pick out an aigrette to go with this dress."

On the shelf is a row of feathered hair clips of the highest quality, all from Maggie's of course. It's easy to see the one that will go best with the blue dress.

Long grayish-blue feathers, wispy and soft.

"Hurry up, Phoebs. We don't want to miss any of the fireworks," Bonnie calls.

I say nothing.

"Phoebe," she says again, staring at me as if I've gone mad.

I'm as frozen as a piece of ice, apparently unable to choose that which is so obvious.

"Phoebe," she says, louder, hands on her hips. "It's not that hard. I can see from here. That one." She's pointing to the bluish-feathered clip.

I hand her the aigrette.

It is ugly. All of them lined up on the shelf are ugly. For I've seen a great blue heron's feathers fluttering in the breeze, attached to a live bird, wild and free. Those feathers are the beautiful ones. Not these dead ones on a shelf that will be worn on a woman's head.

The clip is in her hair now. Bonnie gestures to the shelf. "Help yourself," she says.

The sisters are fiddling with dress bows and their hair. They don't notice that I don't take one. But soon I'm pulled back into their world. It's getting dark. The fireworks will be starting soon.

On our way outside I see Mother and Father dancing in the ballroom. Paulie is sitting in a chair, fidgeting. He holds out his arms when he sees me. I make sure Mother knows I'm taking him off to the fireworks with us.

My parents have not lost their magic on the dance floor. Others have noticed it too. It will not be long before they'll have the floor to themselves. That's how it always is. Other dancers will soon step back to watch. Tonight is no exception.

It's not long before red, white, and blue fireworks begin to explode in the black sky. Sparks trail down and shower out in big wide arches. I hope Jed can see them from wherever he may be.

I look back, up into the ballroom's windows. I can see my parents are watching too. Mother is leaning back into Father's arms. I only have to turn around to see for myself the fireworks. I cannot.

Mother's smile is as bright as a star. Nothing can be more beautiful than that.

TWENTY

A FEW DAYS LATER MOTHER is reading outside, and I am pulling weeds from the garden. It's a warm, windy day. We are enjoying this quiet time together. Then Red, Mr. Spencer's dog, all of a sudden begins to bark like mad.

Mr. Spencer comes over and suggests we go inside. Paulie too, who has been at the woodpile with him "helping" to pile up newly cut logs. It is not a suggestion. "Want to find out what's botherin' him so," Mr. Spencer says, pointing to Red.

I help Mother up. She leans into me as a hard wind gust slams against us. She puts her hand to her hair, trying to hold it in. "A wind-do," she says, laughing. Even when she is as fragile as glass and the wind is whipping her hair, Mother is beautiful and, more importantly, in good spirits.

Mr. Spencer has been over a lot these days. There's always something needing to be done. Daisy is in a continual fluster, exceedingly efficient, exceedingly rattled. This delights Mother and me. Daisy must sense that Mr. Spencer is smitten. Mother and I think Daisy is smitten too.

Red, compared to Jed's Mike, is high strung. Part Irish Wolfhound, part German Shepard, Daisy thinks it's his wolfhound side that makes him uppity. "Probably just the wind that's getting him," she says, as we come up onto the porch. "Can set anyone on edge, high up here on the cliff."

"Wind Cliff," I say, thinking that might be a good name for the cabin.

"Hmmmm," Mother says.

"Cliff Tops," says Daisy.

Mother "hmmms" again.

"Hmmms" are not no's. "Hmmms" mean she wants to think about it some more. "A name has to fit like the last piece of a jigsaw puzzle. It will come with a definite satisfaction that it is the right one," she tells us.

I don't think "Wind Cliff" or "Cliff Tops" will pass the test. There's too much hmmm-ing about them.

Paulie wants to go with Mr. Spencer and Red to check around the place. He's like a puppy, always trailing along at Mr. Spencer's heels. Mr. Spencer says no. I can tell Paulie is trying to be grown-up and not cry. "Come on, Red," Mr. Spencer calls. Red refuses to go outside with him. "That's odd," he says.

No one can call Mr. Spencer talkative. He doesn't force Red to go. He twirls one end of his mustache starting under his nose and by the time his fingers have worked their way to the very end of it, he says, "I have it."

I suppose he means he has a plan.

He reaches up to where he stores his rifle on pegs above the door and pulls it down. "Be right back," he says.

Inside, Red lies down. Then he gets up and paces around the cabin. Sits. Lies down again. Up. Paces some more. He's making us all feel on edge.

Fifteen minutes later Mr. Spencer is back. "Can't for the life of me find what's got that dog so addled."

"Well then, Jack," Mother says, "I hope this means you'll stay for dinner. See if Red will settle in a bit."

"Obliged, ma'am, Thank you."

I like it when Mr. Spencer stays for dinner. Mother and I watch Daisy smile. It's like Mother and I are on the same page, reading the same words. And right now it's all about Daisy and Mr. Spencer. There's a lot going on, although little is being said about it. How they feel about each other is beneath the words they speak. Kind of like the way a tip of an iceberg above water is only a small part of the mountain of ice that's underneath the surface. Or like a flower just before it has fully bloomed. They like each other, plain and simple. It's as easy as that. Mother and I both know it.

Daisy serves ham with boiled potatoes in brown gravy, sweet baked beans with maple syrup, mashed turnips, and buttered bread. Blueberry buckle for dessert.

Afterward Mother takes out the first-looks. Mr. Spencer has never seen a stereoscope before. When he puts it to his eyes and sees the pictures, he jumps. This makes us laugh. I'm thinking he saw one of the nudie statues in Europe, but he says, "Magnificent. The Grand Canyon. I want to see that one day." He's looking at Daisy as he says this.

"Me too," says Daisy. She's letting her guard down, blooming in the rays of Mr. Spencer's kindness and warmth. In that moment, something changes between Daisy and Mr. Spencer.

Mother flashes me a wink.

After we've gone through all the pictures, Mr. Spencer announces it's time to clean his gun.

"Daisy, will you put a kettle on the cookstove please and bring me a pan," he asks.

"'Course, Jack," she answers.

I look at Mother. We caught it. This is the first time she's called him Jack instead of Mr. Spencer.

Mr. Spencer slides two stools in front of the fire. He gestures for Paulie to sit in one. Paulie's eyes are as wide as saucers, riveted on the rifle in Mr. Spencer's lap.

"A good piece needs to be taken care of," he begins. "Its

insides get damp from being outside in all kinds of weather. Powder smoke gets stuck along the barrel's sides too. First we need to take this long ramrod from its holding place under the barrel and tie a clean rag onto its end."

Mr. Spencer stands the rifle upright in the pan Daisy has brought him. Next he pours water from the boiling kettle down the barrel. Paulie is on his feet now. Mr. Spencer makes him stand far back from the hot water. Paulie inches closer. Again Mr. Spencer moves him back with his arm. Paulie is slowing things down, but Mr. Spencer is patient with him.

Then Mr. Spencer takes the ramrod with the rag tied to its end and plunges it into the gun barrel. Brings it up and down. He lets Paulie have a turn, but keeps his hand on the ramrod because hot, black, dirty water spurts out the hole in which the cap is placed when the gun is loaded. This goes on until the water that comes out of the hole is clear.

Mr. Spencer takes another clean rag, greases it lightly before attaching it to the ramrod, and then lets Paulie plunge it down the barrel. A third rag, and Mr. Spencer rubs the rifle all over until it is sleek and shiny.

Mother has lost interest. Guns bore her. She is tired. I help her to bed. "Watching Daisy and Jack, that was the center ring's entertainment of the evening," she says. I kiss her goodnight.

I liked watching Mr. Spencer clean his rifle. I get so mad at Mother's tuberculosis. I wish it could be taken out of her, strung up on a bull's eye and shot at with a rifle. I'd pay more attentions to rifles if I could kill an illness with it.

When I get back to the main room, Daisy is still rapt by the goings on at the hearth. Red, it seems, is quite content to settle when we are all inside with him.

Mr. Spencer is loading the gun now with a bullet he's pulled from a buckskin pouch attached to his belt. "After each shot," he explains, "I have to reload the gun; measure the powder, put it in, shake it down, load the bullet, pound it down, put a fresh cap under the hammer – all before I can take another shot. Best to kill clean on the first shot. A wounded animal can kill a hunter before he has time to reload."

A wounded animal is like an illness's relapse. A hunter thinks he's got it, but he doesn't.

"Well, Mr. Spencer, I mean Jack, you must be an awfully good first shot," Daisy says.

"I aim to be," he answers. The ends of his mustache are twitching. I can't tell if he's blushing from Daisy's compliment or if the heat of the fire in the hearth is making his face red.

Mr. Spencer gets up to leave. Red is agitated. "I need to figure out what's botherin' him," he says.

This time Mr. Spencer takes Red with him. The barking starts immediately. Mr. Spencer knocks on the door, hard and fast.

"Confound it," he says when Daisy opens it. "I can't see what's addlin' Red so. Daisy, promise me that no one will go outside until I've had a chance to come back at sunrise and find out what the dickens is going on."

Daisy is on the receiving end of an order. If Mr. Spencer weren't so serious it'd be funny.

"Swear to me, Daisy," he insists, "that no one will leave this cabin until after I've had a chance to check on things in the light of day."

"Mr. Spencer," (not Jack I notice) "I won't swear to anything, but we are not foolish either. No one will leave until after you have returned."

It is enough. Mr. Spencer gives Daisy a look that says he wanted her to swear. Daisy returns the look with one of her own that says never.

It will have to do.

PHOEBE GREER
Ridge, Colo

LISBETH BURNS
10 July (late), 1900

Dear Lisbeth,

It's only been a few days since you've left Pinedale, and things have gotten batty around here. The man I told you about, Mr. Spencer, who built our cabin, is smitten with Daisy. He is around a lot, checks on us daily, and tonight he has ordered us not to leave our cabin until he comes and gives us an all clear in the morning.

You see, his dog Red went bonkers earlier today. He would not stop barking and couldn't settle until we were all inside. Mr. Spencer thinks there may be an injured animal lurking near here.

The howling wind isn't helping. A witch must be stirring her valley-sized cauldron below, causing frenzied curls of vapor to rise and pummel against us. There's nothing to block the force of such strong gusts up here. It's impossible to sleep. Will tell all on the morrow.

11 July, 1900

Oh Lisbeth. Beyond awful. Truly you can't imagine. We live in a wild place. I saw and smelled it all. Everything.

Red's barking woke me. It was early, the sky tinged with orange. And the smell. There was a horrible stench that went through my nose and on into my windpipes, making me gag. Even if Paulie didn't seem to be bothered by it, I was forced to cover my mouth and nose with a handkerchief.

From our window in the loft, Paulie and I saw Red pawing a mound of branches, leaves, and twigs next to a boulder just behind the ice-house. Mr. Spencer was holding Red by the collar. A minute later he was at the front door. Daisy let him in.

Paulie and I listened from the top of the stairs. He told Daisy that a mountain lion's kill was cached in the mound of brush. When a big cat, as Mr. Spencer calls a mountain lion, kills an elk or a deer, it can't eat it all at once. So the cat hides the carcass, stores the remains somewhere for when he's hungry again. It's called caching. The wind was so strong last night that the death smell was carried away from us. Except Red smelled it. And this morning I smelled it. Ew!

All Paulie wanted to know was if Mr. Spencer was going to use his gun. "Reckon so," he said.

We waited through the morning inside while Mr. Spencer, armed with his rifle, sat on top of the ice-house. He hoped the wind would carry his scent away from the mountain lion, but there was no telling from what direction the animal would approach.

Paulie all of a sudden possessed a great deal of patience. He was frozen to our loft window. An hour later he whispered for me to come up. I wish I hadn't gone up, but I did. I saw the entire grisly event from start to finish.

A mountain lion and her cub came back for their food. Immediately what came to mind was the time it would take for Mr. Spencer to reload his rifle after one shot. He was going to need two shots, at least. And injured animals are dangerous!

They were beautiful, Lisbeth. Sleek, honey-colored, muscular, and wild. The mother cat's only mistake was in picking the wrong place to cache her kill.

Of course I understood what had to be done. It would have been foolish for us to ignore the threat these wild creatures posed for us. Still, that didn't make things easier.

I also understand better now what Jed meant when he spoke about good hunters not being bloodthirsty but having a purpose for their killing. I suppose it's that way for him, killing birds for their feathers. Mr. Spencer didn't want any glory for killing these magnificent animals. He had to. That's all.

After the bullet struck her, the mother lion leapt into the

air with one blood-curdling yelp that raised goose pimples on my arms. It was a good clean shot. Death came fast. A few twitches, then nothing, lifeless.

The cub didn't want to leave its mother. Mr. Spencer's second shot wasn't as accurate as the first. It hit the cub, but it sent him scrambling into the pines, leaving a trail of blood. Mr. Spencer swore. I did too.

"It won't survive long," he said later.

Paulie wanted to go and look for the cub. Mr. Spencer said no. "Look for the crows circling. You'll know it's dead then."

Mr. Spencer carted off the remains of the dead animals, the mountain lion and her cache. We saw the crows about five hours later beneath us, circling near the bottom of the cliff. The cub hadn't made it far. The thought of the little one bleeding and dying slowly and alone during the day is almost too much to bear.

Perhaps I'm not as fit for this wilderness as I thought. What I saw is seared in my brain forever. I can't erase it. Oh, Lisbeth, why in ever did I look?

Missing you and the great city of Denver, your friend,
Phoebe

TWENTY-ONE

IT'S BEEN ALMOST TWO weeks since I saw Jed at the bell ringing. He must be busy hunting with his Pa.

I've been drawing a lot, sitting on our rock, the rock, in the hope that he and Mike will come along. Even with the same view in front of me day after day, there's always something new to see. The question-mark curve of the creek is lined with big boulders, tall pines, aspens, and summer flowers, now in full bloom.

I'm working on an aspen tree. It's hard to get the exact line of a leaf's stem. That's important because if it's not right then the leaf isn't poised for twirling, and that's what makes it special.

A black streak laces through the pines above the trail.

"Mike! Mike!" I shout.

He stops when he hears his name and bounds toward me, ears flopping, exuberant.

"How's your Ma?" Jed asks after jumping onto to the rock.

"Okay," I say. I almost tell him about her dancing at Pinedale, but I think of the last time he was there, stolen cookies in hand, face smeared white, and with unpleasant Mr. Jasper.

"Okay," I say again.

Sometimes it's better to just let things be. It's not wrong or bad to choose not to say something. I don't ask how the plume hunting is going. His clothes are dirty and more tattered than ever. His game bag is empty. I don't have to ask. I offer him a sandwich. He devours it.

While he's eating, I decide not to tell him about the mountain lion incident. He'd understand of course. He's a hunter, but I'm not sure he'd feel the same deep sadness about the whole thing as much as I do. It's not something I want to talk about or explain.

"Be right back," he says. "Mike, stay."

Mike does as he's told, but his eyes follow Jed's every move.

Jed is picking wildflowers. The sun is warm. It reflects dazzling water-stars off Bear Creek, which, today, is flowing in a trickle-whisper. Jed brings me a bouquet. "For yur Ma," he says.

Blue-violet columbines. Daisies. Orange Indian paintbrush. Simply beautiful. I dampen the sandwich cloth in the creek and wrap it around the bunched stems. "She'll love these. Thank you."

Jed lost his own mother. His asking about mine is his way of saying that he knows it must be hard to have a very sick mother, of saying he can feel my hurt, even if he doesn't use those exact words. What isn't said can be as telling as what is.

Jed has too much energy to sit still for long. "Come on, Phoebe. Let's climb a tree. I know the perfect one. We kin look for a great blue's nest. They nest high. Kin be hard t'find. If we see a nest, the bird ain't far away."

Until that moment I'd forgotten about the great blue heron I'd seen right from this very rock.

He'd want to know.

I'll tell him later.

Maybe.

Jed gives me a hard look, as if he knows I'm keeping a secret. He's a hunter and, I think, must be alert to things even before he knows what they are or can see them.

Thankfully his high-spiritedness gets the best of him.

He's already jumped onto the bank and is running on the trail. "Come on, Fancy Pants. Hurry, up!" he shouts.

They are fancy I think, and I'm delighted to be wearing them. I tuck the flowers in my drawing satchel and leave it on the bank after jumping from the rock, which I can do easily now. When I get to the tree Jed wants to climb, he is already standing on a low branch.

""Tis a good one," he says, tapping the branch with his foot. "I'll help ya'. Put yer foot there, on that rock, and take a step up. Branches nottin' but rungs on a ladder."

I don't hesitate. If Jed believes I can do something, I know it can be done.

I haven't been on many ladders, but slowly, branch-by-branch, we make our way up. There's a rhythm to climbing a tree. I'm not as fast as Jed, but I'm getting the hang of it.

Squirrels cluck. Two are on nearby branches. Mountain squirrels are different than the gray mushroom-colored ones in Denver that no one pays any mind. Here, they're black and have tufts of fur pointing up from the tips of their ears. They've noticed us and by the sound of them I'm guessing they don't want to be bothered.

Whatever reticence Jed sometimes has when his feet are on the ground, up here in the trees, it is gone. It's as if being high in a tree frees him to be himself. I know the feeling. It's like that when I'm drawing, when I'm me the most.

Jed seems to have no fear of falling. Casually he takes one hand off the tree's branch to point to various places he wants me to see. "And there's me and Pa's cabin. Over there," and now he's pointing in the opposite direction, "be the wild raspberry patch the bears love in August. And look, Phoebe," he says pointing at the sky, "a day moon."

It's hard to keep up with him. I'm still looking at the ramshackle and decrepit cabin where he and his Pa live. It's nothing like the cabin Mr. Spencer built for us. If Jed's Ma were still alive, I doubt she would have stood for that cabin looking like nobody cared for it. Jed and his Pa care only for hunting. He's told me they move around a lot. Have to be where the hunting is good.

I'm catching up to the raspberry patch and the day moon, trying to keep my balance on the branch.

"Moon's not as far away as you'd think," he says, still holding onto the branch above him with one hand.

"You're a monkey," I say.

He takes both hands and, balancing on the branch with just his feet, he curls them under his arms and shouts a loud "ooo-ooo!" He throws his head back and shakes it wildly. He wobbles a bit, but unconcerned, he takes hold of the branch again with one hand as if it's for nothing more than to move it slightly in order to get a better view of the moon.

"Daredevil!"

He laughs. I thought we came up here to look for a heron's nest and that that would be a serious and quiet undertaking. Apparently not. Looking for a nest seems to be the farthest thing from his mind.

The outside world belongs to Jed, and like an elk, a mountain lion, a black fox brushed silver with a white-tipped tail, and yes, like a great blue heron, he belongs to it. He's part of something wild and magnificent, a world in which he feels safe, a place, though harsh, is also wonderfully alive. No one can ever take this from him. Jed can never lose it because it is in him. It's who he is. And he's sharing it all with me.

I receive all of this. It is the finest gift in the world. Jed and his Pa don't have much money, but what he's giving me is beyond any price.

Seeing the world through his eyes opens up something in me. I'm alert in a new way, a way that could never exist in me in Denver. Nature's boldness, its raw beauty, which I can now see, thanks to Jed, demands its place in my drawings.

"Thank you," I whisper.

He gives me the widest, goofiest, most freckle-fusing smile I've ever seen.

TWENTY-TWO

ATHER IS HOME WHEN I return. I give Mother the flowers. Tell her they are from Jed.

"What have you been doing, Phoebe?" Father asks, his voice stern, He pulls a twig from my hair. "Your clothes are ripped and mud-stained. Give me your hands, young lady."

When Father calls me "young lady," this usually means I'm in for it. Palms up, I give him my hands. He turns them over, frowning at the lines of dirt under my nails.

"Climbing trees," I explain.

"With that lay-about, good-for-nothing plume hunter?" He doesn't wait for an answer. "I don't want you running around with a scoundrel like that. Your Mother and I are working hard to bring you up as a lady."

My jaw tightens. I look at the bouquet of flowers in

Mother's hand. Didn't Father hear me when I told her they were from Jed?

"Robert," says Mother. Her voice is sad, but there is strength in it, too. And a warning. Father will not want to upset her by having a row with me.

An ugly silence builds between Father and me. Even though it is invisible, it's there all the same, as solid and sure as the cliff upon which our cabin is built.

Later, during dinner, Father announces he's decided that I'm going with him back to Denver for the week. I'll be staying with Lisbeth. This was supposed to be a happy surprise. Indeed, when I first arrived here at the beginning of the summer, I would have jumped at the chance to leave Ridge and spend a week with Lisbeth in Denver.

And even right after the mountain lion killing, I had found myself thinking I would rather be back in Denver. That incident was heart-wrenching for all of us. But there wasn't any other way it could have been handled.

But time has passed.

After today, having spent time with Jed in the tree, to tell the truth, I'm not excited to go. I'd rather stay here. Given Father's mood, though, and being told I'm going to Denver with him, I must say it feels more like being sentenced to prison, as if I were being banished to the city for doing something wrong. To Father's mind, my crime, I think, must be having a friend like Jed.

No matter. I'm going. I know better than to argue a decision that Father has already made.

Denver.

In spite of not being all that eager about coming, now that I'm here, it's like returning to a comfortable pair of old slippers. I miss Ridge, Jed, and especially Mother, but Lisbeth is pulling me into her spinning-whirl of activities, and they're not unpleasant in the slightest.

Swept along in the blizzard of wedding plans for her sister Bonnie, we go to teas in her honor, dress fittings, and shopping for the trousseau – twelve of everything, from plates to face cloths. Even my parents, who are used to nice things and a comfortable lifestyle, might think all of this excessive and showy.

When I think about what Father said about Jed, I get mad. He'd prefer that I spend time with people like Lisbeth and the daughters of his railroad magnate friends, wealthy men like my father who worked hard to raise money for the expanding railroad lines spidering across the country. And Mother came from a moneyed family. She was a debutante. She and Father are listed – along with Paulie and me – in the social registrar, "the stud book" Daisy calls it. Inherited wealth and lineage is important to Father; less so for Mother, but she must appreciate the advantages of money. After all, my parents had enough money that they could make the choice between putting Mother in a sanatorium for sick people near Denver or building her a cabin in the mountains.

I'm getting a lifetime supply of Denver society this week. I like it plenty, perhaps because in seven days it will be over. Daisy says that small, short doses of anything are better than an overdose, which reminds me of the time Lisbeth and I once ate an entire cake in one sitting. Afterward, I felt sick.

Today we are at Maggie's, "Denver's Finest Millinery," as the sign on the window says. Hats in every imaginable style decorate the showroom. They sit on wax heads, complete with glass eyes. Custom-made hats. Expensive hats. On shelves under glass countertops are aigrettes, fans made with owl feathers, and eye masks.

Massive chandeliers hang from the ceiling. Sunlight spills into the showroom through large windows. The store itself has been described as a work of art. But maybe because Ridge is so beautiful too, Maggie's strikes me in a new way today, not as grand or impressive as I once thought it to be.

Lisbeth and I are "working" with Edgar, trying to teach him to cuss. His cage sits at the top of a pedestal in the middle of the showroom. Edgar is at least three feet long from crest to tail feathers. His breast is a rich gold color, his back a deep sky-blue, bright red on his wings. He replaced the violinist that used to fiddle through the day for customers and clerks. And like Maggie's as a whole, it feels like I'm seeing Edgar for the first time. He strikes me as one of the loneliest and saddest creatures I've ever seen.

Edgar shakes his head, preens a long feather, and stares at us with yellow eyes. He rattles his leg that is attached to his cage by a gold chain. He utters a blood-curdling screech, "SHEET!"

Mr. Burns rushes over and cover's Edgar's cage with a cloth. He is wearing a gray felt bowler that has, as an ornament, a taxidermied hummingbird with diamonds set in its eyes. Lisbeth claps her hands. "Good boy," she says. There is the sound of laughter. A few women walk over to us and ask that Mr. Burns take off Edgar's cloth. I think, secretly he is pleased with Edgar's exhibition, despite his pretending not to be.

Poor bird.

When the ladies lose interest in Edgar, Mr. Burns shoos us away.

Maggie's has many full-length looking glasses. We try on various hats and parade in front of them, pretending to be grand ladies. The store is busy. Mr. Burns doesn't want us flitting about like bothersome flies. He waves us off again.

We go into the back room where the hats are made. Fall

season, Maggie's busiest, is just around the corner. While the showroom's atmosphere is hushed and subdued, Edgar's occasional screech the exception, the backroom is a beehive of activity.

It's almost as big as the showroom, well lit and ventilated by big open windows. An electric wind machine hangs from the ceiling for hot days. Compared to other milliners who sell cheaper products, these are good working conditions. Mr. Burns has the reputation of employing only the best. Many of his workers have been at the store for over fifteen years.

Ladies sit around six large tables, intensely focused on their work. On each table is a mountain of supplies: wire, straw, silk, ribbons, chiffon, artificial flowers, and bird feathers. One designer per table presides over the six or seven woman making the hats. Maggie, the head designer, directs the makers, trimmers, cullers, and sewers in their tasks with the authority and precision of a ship's captain. There is a woman at each table whose sole responsibility is to sort feathers and keep the piles neat.

Lisbeth says that Maggie gets her ideas from the fashion magazines. She steals from the European designers, which is what American women want. Maggie, according to Lisbeth, believes it was Marie Antoinette who, over a century ago, put a peacock feather into her hair, received compliments from the king, and thus started the feather craze in women's hats.

Maggie says her hardest task is to balance the need for speed with the delicacy of touch. Mr. Burns is a businessman. He wants to sell as many hats as quickly as possible, but refuses to settle for anything less that the highest quality. Apparently Maggie is talented and can make good hats fast.

I look at the mound of feathers on the table closest to me. I know where it all starts now: with a bird like the blue heron I saw in Bear Creek, who has no idea of how much money his feathers are worth. If he is at the wrong place at the wrong time – as was the mountain lion and her cub – his feathers will end up on a table like the one in front of me. I feel like I'm in a slaughterhouse, without the blood and guts, but equally as unpleasant.

I don't understand why women want to wear these hats. Perhaps they are waiting for compliments from some faraway king. It makes no sense. There's no rule that says a woman has to follow the current fashion. Yet Maggie's is busy. Very busy, bursting with orders in fact.

Lisbeth is staring at me, wondering, I suppose, why I look so stricken. There are pieces to a puzzle in front of me that I can't put in their rightful places just yet. Her father owns Maggie's. She will not understand if I tell her about seeing a great blue heron, his quiet beauty, and how, in dusk's

violet light, he stood alone in the creek searching for something to eat, his feathers tousled by the wind, and opened
my heart.

TWENTY-THREE

MISS RUBY ARDEAN IS having a sale. Regular fortunes normally cost four dollars. But for the week I'm in Denver, they are only a dollar. Miss Ruby's fortune-tellings are expensive because her parlor is above Maggie's. To get to Miss Ruby's, a customer has to go in through the millinery. Any lady who can afford one of Maggie's hats can afford Miss Ruby's four-dollar fortune-telling. And then every once in a while, she'll have a sale. "Keeps traffic moving," says Mr. Burns. "Good for the both of our businesses."

Lisbeth really wants her fortune read and has pestered her father so much that he finally gives in and hands us each a dollar. I can't decide if I want mine read or not, but I find myself climbing the stairs with Lisbeth to Miss Ruby's.

We wait in her front room on chairs covered with striped

red-and-pink fabric, better suited for an ice-cream parlor I think. It is a hot day. Ridge never gets as hot as Denver. For a moment I long to be back there, on the rock in Bear Creek, dangling my feet in the icy mountain water.

"Be right there, girls," calls Miss Ruby from behind a curtain.

Lisbeth cannot sit still. She's bouncing her knees up and down like she always does in school when she's not listening to the teacher. She can't wait for Miss Ruby to tell her about her future. Lisbeth doesn't have a sick mother.

Miss Ruby walks out from behind the curtain. It's easy to see that she once was a beautiful woman. She still is, but she is no longer young, or thin, but she isn't fat either. Something wild, barely contained, lurks under her calm demeanor. I can't help wondering, where has she been in this world? What secrets she carries deep within her.

She is wearing a red scarf around her head. Gray wispy hairs spring out from under the scarf, framing her round face. Big golden hoop earrings dangle from her ears. As she walks, a deep maroon-colored skirt with gold threads woven throughout it swirls around her.

Lisbeth is on her feet in an instant, but Miss Ruby is watching me. I meet her gaze. She has beautiful green eyes that match the color of her bright blouse. Lisbeth will not stop prattling on and on. She is insistent for Miss Ruby's attention.

Miss Ruby sighs and switches her focus to Lisbeth, as if surrendering to her is easier than opposing her. They disappear behind the curtain.

I lose track of time. The sounds of the city seem so far away. All of a sudden Lisbeth is nudging me. "Wake up, Phoebe. Miss Ruby is reading our fortunes for free. She's letting us keep our dollars. We mustn't tell Father. We'll get some candy with it later. Except she's not using her cards or her crystal ball. Says we are too young. She'll read your palm though. She just did mine."

Lisbeth holds out her palms as if seeing them for the first time. She is beaming.

"Do you want a turn, Phoebe?" Miss Ruby asks.

I'm about to say no thank-you, but when I look into Miss Ruby's green eyes, I know I'm going to have my palm read. The battle between wanting to know and not wanting to know is over in an instant. She holds out her hand to me. I take it and follow her.

Behind the curtain is a small room, simply furnished with a table, lamp, and two chairs. On a shelf I see a crystal ball and a stack of cards. A kerosene-fed wind machine makes a noise that muffles all conversation behind the curtain to those sitting in the outside parlor. It explains the droning noise that probably lulled me to sleep while I was waiting for Lisbeth.

A block of ice sits in a porcelain bowl in front of the machine. The wind machine's spinning blades put forth a steady stream of cool ice-tinged air aimed right at us. It feels good. Crystals hanging from the lampshade jingle in the gentle whirl of air.

"Phoebe," Miss Ruby is saying, "you and Lisbeth are the youngest customers I've ever had. A palm reading is fine for you both, but I will not use my ball or cards. Too much is written in them. You are at an age where it's important to write your own story."

She holds out her hand. I put my hand in hers, palm up. With her finger, she traces the lines on my palm. I'm scared to find out what she sees. I blurt it out. "Is my mother going to die?" It is a bold question. And now that I've asked it, I want an answer. "Yes or no?" I say.

"I can't answer that, Phoebe," she answers.

I'm mad. "Why not?" I demand. If Miss Ruby had taken my dollar I would have insisted she give it back.

"Because every question doesn't always have an answer. And difficult questions rarely have simple answers. But people who ask them have courage. They understand that life can be hard."

Miss Ruby's eyes seem sad. Perhaps her life hasn't been

easy? I wonder if she has a child? Fortune-tellers are supposed to tell other people about themselves, but I sense some things about Miss Ruby. I believe she is kind. I think I can trust her. Like me, she doesn't know if Mother will get well. She's not sugar coating or promising anything just to make me feel good. I like that.

When she says, "Let me tell you what I *can* see," I'm ready to hear what she has to say.

Her voice has softened. I lean in. I'm being pulled in under her spell, willingly.

Her voice is silky and deep. "Before me sits a compassionate, sensitive, and determined young lady. There's a flicker of something in you that I don't see often. A desire to give something of yourself to the world. It's right here," she says, taking her finger from my palm and tapping my heart.

"You must wait." She is still studying my palm intently. "Be patient to see how that desire will take form. It's in your heart." She looks up, catching my eyes and holding them. "Beware too, for hearts can break. Don't let a heart that's split in two cave in on itself. This would ruin the dance beginning to form inside of you." She looks down again, clasping my hand in hers.

"Remember," she concludes, her hands warm and firm, cupping my hand like it were a small bird in a nest, "anything worthwhile comes with pain. That's how you know it's meaningful."

I have no idea what Miss Ruby is saying, but I like the idea of a dance forming in my heart. She is done. I suppose she has given me a dollar's worth to think about. There's something in my heart like a dance, not yet fully formed, but it will be one day. And when that happens, I can give it to the world. That is something!

Later Lisbeth tells me what Miss Ruby told her. Her palm reading was as unlike mine as night is to day. She'll have many suitors, more than Bonnie ever had, which delights her, lots of children, domestic bliss. According to Lisbeth, undoubtedly it was the most golden-colored future Miss Ruby has ever unearthed.

Thankfully Lisbeth doesn't ask me about my session with Miss Ruby.

More than anything, Miss Ruby left me with hope, that there is something I have yet to discover about myself that will somehow make a difference in the world. I cannot imagine what that might be, but I'll be ready for it.

It's scary not knowing. Not knowing about Mother, not knowing what my purpose will be, but that's okay. For now, I must be patient. Relief pours through me. Thank goodness my fortune wasn't anything like Lisbeth's.

TWENTY-FOUR

MRS. BURNS IS GOING to take us to tea at the Brown Palace Hotel! When I tell her that I didn't pack a nice-enough dress, she says to borrow one from Lisbeth. I suggest that Father can bring one over. Mrs. Burns surprises me by saying that he's gone back to Ridge. Mother is not doing well.

My heart sinks. I try not to panic. I've been living with Mother's ups and downs now for a long time. I don't trust the good spells to last and have learned to endure the bad ones. I wish Father had told me himself.

Mrs. Burns is a bit of a fortune-teller too. She read my thoughts. "He didn't want to worry you," she says.

Luckily Lisbeth and I are the same size. She has lots of dresses from which to choose. Any of them will do. I take the first one I touch. Like all the others, mine as well, it is full of troublesome tiny buttons that take forever to do and undo.

If outside the Brown Palace is dust, cattle, cowboys, saloons, gambling dens, and the occasional gunshot, all of which, minus the gunshot, we pass by on our way there, inside is an oasis of elegance and charm. The hotel takes up the space of an entire city block. On one of its corners, 17th and Larimer, it comes to a point, like the prow of a ship. The cost of a room for the night is astronomical, a whole five dollars.

The hotel's saloon is a man's place. I've been there with Father once. We were walking by and he wanted to give me a peek. It isn't the type of place I should be lingering, even with him, but I remember it well. An arched swordfish hangs on the dark oak wall above the liquor bottles.

A ship's wheel stands at the entrance. According to Father, everyone touches it. We both put our hands on it. He said people like taking the helm of a ship. It's a way of taking charge.

It must be hard to command a ship over a great surging ocean. More often than not, I bet the ocean gets the upper hand. Depends, Father said. A good captain can navigate through bad weather and come out fine.

Father laughed when I reminded him that the Brown Palace was nowhere near an ocean. Perhaps it's here, in this

WINNIE ANDERSON

bar that has a swordfish hanging in it and a ship's wheel at its entrance, that Father gets his notions of sea legs. The memory makes me think of being lost at sea. I feel my life spinning out of control.

Maybe Father should have Mr. Spencer build us a ship's wheel at the entrance to our cabin in Ridge. See if it has the power to set us to rights. See if it helps us to chart a course through the roughest of storms. See if we can come out fine at the far end of a bad spell.

The tearoom, though, where I am now sitting, is a place for the ladies. Located in the center atrium of the hotel, there are twelve floors above it. A massive chandelier hangs from the ceiling. Two tables have been pushed together. I am one of a large crowd: Mrs. Burns, Bonnie, a few of her friends and their mothers, Lisbeth and me. I'm the only one without a mother.

I resist the urge to rise from the table and flee to Ridge to be with Mother. I can't. I'll ruin Bonnie's party if I demand that Mrs. Burns take me to the train station. Then there's the long stage ride to Ridge. I'd have to figure all that out for myself. I don't want to cause my parents more worry than they already have. I take a deep breath and stay seated.

The tea is in Bonnie's honor. Her wedding is in September. The wedding party will take place here, after the ceremony. Today is for making plans and sampling hors d'oeuvres.

Tea is served in fancy white-and-gold bone china cups with roses painted on them. Multi-tiered silver serving plates with an array of cucumber, cheese, and watercress sandwiches laid out on doilies are brought to our tables. They are good, but the petit-fours are better.

Daisy holds to strange ideas about not wanting Paulie and me to eat too much sugar. She's not here, thankfully.

I'm fidgety. All this wedding talk is beginning to bore me. But it clearly fascinates Lisbeth.

Her dress is pinching me. I can't lean back in my chair because of the long snake of buttons running down the dress's back. Honestly, is it women who are designing these fashions? It's hot. Waiters hover close with trays of petit-fours. I take one, then another with my other hand, and sit up as straight as I can, as I must in that dress.

My attention wanders to a group of ladies sitting next to us. Something is different about them, but I can't figure out what it is exactly. Daisy's probably right about the sugar. I've had so much that I can't think straight.

Like every other lady here they are fashionably dressed. Except, ah, now I see it! Not one of them is wearing feathered millinery. That's it. Two of them have nothing on their heads. The third wears a jeweled clip in her hair. It reflects light from the chandelier. When she tilts her head, it sparkles.

I can't hear what they are saying, but there is an intense conversation going on between them. I'm curious. What in the world are they talking about? I'm guessing it's not about an upcoming wedding.

Lisbeth elbows me. "Stop staring, Phoebe," she barks, a nasty edge in her tone. "Mother and Father hate those ladies," she adds in a whisper.

"Why?" I ask, as I'm starting to figure out some things for myself.

"Look at them," she says, as if they were ugly animals in a zoo. "They're making a statement by not wearing feathered hats. There's a group of these women in Denver. Audubon, they call themselves, after the famous bird painter. There are groups of these women forming all over the country. In Boston they are organizing a boycott of bird hats." Lisbeth looks galled, astonished at her own words, as if wondering how in the world could something like that be in the realm of possibility here in Denver.

"They want to protect birds from being used to make hats. Father says this nonsense is making its way west. By the looks of them," Lisbeth sneers, "it has already. Crazy thinking. They'll have a hard time changing the current fashion. Women love bird hats."

That may be true, I think. But how do women come to fasten their love on such things as a dead bird's feathers on a hat or the uncomfortable, back-pinching, tiny buttons on dresses? Maybe this is what Daisy means when she says too many people follow the pack?

"And besides," Lisbeth concludes, "if no one buys feathered millinery, that'll put my father out of business." She stuffs a petit four in her mouth and turns her attention back to her sister and the others at our table.

I don't say anything, but think also of Jed and his Pa. They work hard for not much money. They'll be put out of business too if feather dealers don't pay them because women no longer want to wear feathered hats.

The ladies next to me are pretty. Father once said that a beautiful hat does nothing for an ugly woman. I suppose that wasn't very nice, but he was speaking about Mother. She needs very little adornment. Come to think of it I've never seen Mother with feathers on her head. Never. It surprises me that I haven't noticed that before.

My thinking suddenly turns crystal clear, like the water in Bear Creek. Here's what I believe: the only place feathers look good is on a bird in its natural setting. Taking a bird's life for the purpose of making a hat doesn't make sense. Women who think dead birds on their heads make them pretty need their eyes checked. Maybe if they just see wild birds in their natural setting, like I did when I saw the blue heron in Bear Creek, they'll change their notions about what looks good and what does not.

The thought makes me smile, because it feels like I've settled something for myself. No one at my table notices, in the midst of their chatter, but when I look over, I see the woman who is wearing the jeweled clip in her hair at the neighboring table smile back at me. It's as if she's read my thoughts. For a second I think she might get up and invite me to join her and the other women, but she is only calling for the waiter. Then something one of the other ladies says draws her back into the conversation, and leaves me wishing I were at that table.

TWENTY-FIVE

LATER IN THE WEEK, Father returns to pick me up
at Lisbeth's. We speak little on the trip back to Ridge.
He's worried about Mother. Very worried. While I was at
Lisbeth's, she had a setback. She's coughing up blood now. I
tell Father he should have taken me with him when he went
to Ridge earlier in the week. Mother, he says, wanted me to
have time with Lisbeth. I let the matter drop.

It isn't easy to be around Father when he's so preoccupied
and sad. I'd only disappoint him more if I told him that I
found all the wedding talk one giant bore. I think he assumes
I'm excited about such la-di-da. What I am excited about is
seeing my friend Jed.

The change in Mother is dramatic. She's lost even more
weight. It hurts her to talk so she whispers when she has

something to say. To lesson the pain in her chest now, she sleeps sitting up.

I tell her about my week in Denver. She's eager to hear about the ladies at the Brown Palace who sat next to us.

"It's about time an Audubon group formed in Denver," she says. "They're well-established in places like New York and Boston."

"Lisbeth says that in Boston they are already boycotting millineries. Mr. Burns is worried."

"He should be," Mother says. Even though she is whispering and very tired, Mother's eyes are alert. She wants to talk about this. "You've never seen me in one of those hats. I know first hand that women's club business can be a lot of dither about nothing. But when ladies come together for a set purpose, they will be a voice for change. Women buy those ugly hats. And it's women who need to force fashions to shift away from wearing dead birds and their parts on their head."

"One of Bonnie's friends' mother wore an owl head on her hat," I say.

Mother makes a face. "By rallying against the feather-plume millinery industry and working to protect birds for being slaughtered for their feathers, the Audubon groups have a powerful message."

"A message that's making its way to Denver."

She nods. "And don't forget, young lady, the importance

of a good education. These Audubon ladies are smart and articulate. To speak and write well is a valuable asset. And for you, I'll add drawing. You have talent that one day might be channeled for a greater good."

I like school and especially art classes, but I've never thought of it as a means to something bigger.

"Miss Ruby says that I have a dance in my heart. And that one day I will share it with the world."

"Ah, Miss Ruby. I like that, a dance in your heart. That's a perfect way to describe something you love to do."

"A dance in my heart," I repeat, still not sure what kind of dance is taking shape in me.

Mother is drifting off to sleep. She takes my hand. Hers feels so fragile. "I would have loved sitting with those Audubon ladies, you know."

"Me too," I say, and then I sit with her until she falls asleep.

TWENTY-SIX

WHILE I WAS IN Denver, Father began a project. He's building an outside dance floor in the middle of a small aspen grove on our land for Mother. Paulie is helping him. They spend as much time as they can working on it.

When Mother was well, my parents used to go to dance parties at the Brown Palace. There, in the Casanova Room, they'd waltz, dip, and even tango until well into the night. I may have a kind of dance in my heart, but Miss Ruby only used that phrase as a way to suggest I had something in me – not necessarily an actual dance – that I will one day give the world. Everybody must have a dance of one sort or another inside of him or her.

Mother and Father however have a real dance in their hearts. And in their feet. And with each other. Together they are beautiful dancers.

I'm not sure why Father is beginning this project now, of all times. Perhaps it's his way of taking the ship wheel, of wanting to be at the helm, as the surging ocean threatens to overpower all those fighting against its strength. Building a dance floor now is hope. Father will not give up. I hear the hammer morning, noon, and night. Bang. Bang. Bang. It never stops.

And Mother likes the idea of it too. It doesn't matter, how strong the ocean is or that it might one day drown them. What matters is that Father is fighting against it – for her. I think she likes the hammering noise.

I tell Father I'm going for a walk. I have my drawing pad with me. I want to see Jed too. I haven't seen him for a week. I'm hopeful that he and Mike will come along down Bearberry Trail. I'm eager to get to our rock.

Father's words cut sharp and deep, taking me by surprise. "You're not going to see that good-for-nothing hunter? Ted, is it? Climbing trees, Phoebe. I won't have my daughter turning into a local rag-tag rapscallion."

I had been expecting a nod, perhaps a wave, kinder words like "Have a good time, Phoebe."

I'm as angry as I've ever been. "I hope I do see him!" I shout. "Jed! Jed! Jed is his name!"

I want to say more, like how Jed always asks about Mother, how high-society Lisbeth never does, that he's caught a fish bare-handed for Mother, picked her a bouquet, is so nice to Paulie, but most of all that's he's my friend, which is reason enough to get his name right and to stop the insults.

Except that I want to get away more. I storm off, half expecting Father to run after me, grab my arm, and forbid me to go. He does not.

I go to the rock, try to skip stones on the water's surface, and make an attempt to finish my drawing of the great blue heron standing in the middle of the creek. I pretty much have the heron done. I just need to finish his world, the curve of the creek, the flowers on its bank, the aspen and pine trees, and the boulders. But I cannot settle. I'm too upset by Father's words. I don't want Jed to see me like this. I have to do something and be alone, really alone.

The tree is much easier to climb this time. Pine branches rustle in the wind. Their smell is calming. The sun shines warm in a blue, blue sky. It doesn't take long before I'm much higher than I was with Jed.

I'm on a sturdy branch, secure, leaning in against the tree's thick trunk. I close my eyes. Focus on the silence around me. The quiet fades away. It's a matter of letting go of one language and tuning into another. The roar of the creek. Whispering pines. A squirrel's cluck. A woodpecker's tap, tap, tap.

I'm pulled out of myself and into this other world, where

beauty and harshness exist, as different pieces in the same puzzle. For a brief moment I am part of this world too. I belong here, high in a tree, alone but not lonely, as much as a shining star belongs in a black sky.

I wish Mother were with me. I wish she'd get healthy. I wish it weren't so hard for Father and me all the time. I want to see Jed soon. I wish things didn't have to be so hard for him. So many wishes.

A high-pitched whistle brings me back into myself. I open my eyes and look straight down into the elbow curve of the Bear Creek, where again, there is a great blue heron standing in the shallows.

He walks deliberately and slowly, intent. Then he stops, bends low so that his chest and neck are near the water. Coiling his long neck into a tight S shape, his head dives into the water. He comes up with a fish in his bill. Straightening his neck, he wriggles it slightly, tilts his head up, and jerks the fish up into the air before catching it vertically in his bill. I see the fish's shape in his neck as it goes down.

Satisfied now, he unrolls his wings and begins to fly, awkwardly, trying to get airborne. His legs pump up and down and back and forth. If Jed were with me, this is when he'd take his shot. "No," I whisper.

But Jed isn't here and everything is coming together, and the great blue is flying toward me, as if he wants me to see him, gracefully now, on big magnificent wings. With each deep wingbeat his body rocks rhythmically up and down.

He passes right by me, his silver undersides plainly visible. Peering yellow eyes stare into me, laying his trust bare. I could have reached out and touched him. His swoosh of air brushes tendrils of hair across my face. He perches on a nearby branch of a neighboring tree and screeches a loud guttural squawk. His head jerks. He cocks it toward me and squawks again.

His mate calls back to him from their nest. Ah, so there it is!

I sense how fragile all living creatures are and understand his fierce desire to protect his mate. What if he loses her? What if Mother does not get better this time? I feel my father's heartbreak, and my sadness. Together, they are as vast and as big as the universe. My eyes fix on the great blue herons, perched so near me, each so keenly aware of the other. I'd like to tell the great blues that I see their world and because of that, I understand my own a little bit better.

He flies off. His mate quiets into their nest.

I cry. I cannot help it. My tears are like the spring snowmelt off Mt. Veil, roaring down the canyon, gathering strength. They will never stop. My tears can fill an ocean. But there is also a sense of relief in my tears, and, perhaps, even a tiny flicker of joy. For the great blue has put his life in my hands.

My nose drips. I snort. And when I've completely cried myself out, I climb down the tree. I know one thing as sure as sure can be. I will never betray this bird's trust. I cannot and will not give his life away by telling Jed the whereabouts of his nest.

TWENTY-SEVEN

D ANG! I LEFT MY sketchbook on the rock. When I go back to get it, Jed is there, flipping through its pages. My heart sinks. I'm tempted to flee. I was so excited to see him. Now I'm afraid. He's seen my drawing of the great blue heron.

He does not smile or wave when he sees me.

Mike trots to my side, tail wagging. He nudges his head into my side, wanting a scratch between his ears. Mike must sense Jed's reserve. He keeps looking back at his master, who has jumped onto the bank. Jed hands me my sketchbook.

I can see the pain in his eyes. His shoulders hunch forward. It's like all of his usual energy has drained out of him. Hunters have good instincts. He's figured out that I've known about a great blue heron being in these parts for a while now.

I have the feeling that all my time in Ridge has been leading me to this moment. I must face this. On the outside this is an ordinary late afternoon. Dusk's cold shadows are beginning to spread like ink stains as the sun dips below the mountains.

Inside, my heart is splitting. The hurt in Jed's eyes makes me wish I'd never seen the great blue. I need to grab hold of a ship's wheel. I know now that this is what Miss Ruby meant when she said that doing anything worthwhile takes courage. This is going to hurt, what I'm about to do. The both of us.

I take the sketchbook.

"Ya' see the nest, Phoebe? Do ya' know where it is?"

It'd be so easy to tell Jed everything. I want to see his smile again. I take a deep breath. I'm plowing through a storm of tall waves.

"I can't say."

Silence spreads between us, wider and deeper as each second passes.

"Ya' can," he says. "'Course ya' can, but ya' won't." He stands taller and shakes his head in disgust. "Come on, Mike. Phoebe found a pot o' gold and she ain't sharin'."

They walk away.

I'm lost in the middle of an ocean of loneliness. It takes everything I have not to run after them and tell Jed what he wants to hear. It comes to me that I made my decision long ago, the moment I first saw the blue heron standing in the creek. I knew then that I'd protect him in any way I could. And now I've come face-to-freckly-face with what that decision will cost me.

Jed.

LISBETH BURNS
Denver, Colo

PHOEBE GREER
1 August, 1900

Dear Phoebe,

I wish you hadn't had to leave, knowing that you love the wedding hullabaloo as much as I do. Even now, after so much planning and parties, there's more. More teas! More shopping! More dress fittings! More of everything! Lucky me. You must miss it. How could you not?

Miss Ruby asked about you the other day. She said you were strong. Come to think of it, Phoebs, you never told me what she said about your future. I sure hope it was as wonderful and as sunny as mine. Think of it; marrying the man of our dreams, children, a house to run as we see fit. What in the world could be better than that?

I wish you were here. If I may be so bold, I think your father should put your mother in a sanatorium here in Denver. There are some very nice ones. If he did, we could start school together.

I must run now. Have to take notes for when it's my wedding. I'll take them for you. There's so much to learn.

Friends forever,
Lisbeth

PHOEBE GREER
Ridge, Colo

LISBETH BURNS
10 August, 1900

Dear Lisbeth,

There are a few things you need to know.

First, Mother and Father are the only people who will decide what is best for Mother. Long ago, and with the most respected doctor in Denver, they made the decision to come to the mountains for Mother's health. Not only is she with her family, she is also receiving far better care here in Ridge than she would as an inmate in a sanatorium, no matter how "nice" it is. What is best for Mother is guiding these decisions.

Your suggestion for her to be brought to Denver was selfish. It would have brought me to you, as a plaything. Never once have you asked about her health. Never. It's always about you. You mean well, I suppose, but you need to learn when to keep your mouth shut when it comes to other people's affairs.

I didn't tell you about my session with Miss Ruby because, again, you never asked. Frankly at the time I was grateful, for my fortune wasn't anything like yours. I may have a husband, children, and a house of my own, but there will be something else too, some other purpose to which my heart and soul will belong. Tell Miss Ruby that things are starting to come together, the pieces beginning to fit, even though it hasn't been easy.

I won't be able to go into Maggie's anymore to parade in front of the looking glass with feathered millinery on my head. You see, to put it simply, I've seen, twice now, a most spectacular bird, a great blue heron. He has flown into my heart. And when he came within an arm's reach of me, in flight, I thought he was the most beautiful, wild, and free a creature as I've ever seen.

I hadn't heard of the Audubon club until that day we were in the Brown Palace at tea. I must thank you for that. I've learned that they want laws to protect birds from being slaughtered for their feathers. They believe women's tastes in fashion need to change. I agree with them whole-heartedly.

You may think it a small thing to declare that I can't go into Maggie's anymore. Perhaps it is, but small things make a difference and can lead to something bigger. I know what the gift of a bouquet of wild flowers does for Mother's spirits. I know that Father's building an outside dance floor for

Mother – even now when she's so sick – is not giving up. Hope is not a small thing. Making a difference in your own small way is not a small thing. Big things come from small starts.

Thinking about birds in this way has cost me my plume-hunter friend. He is the most kind and considerate person I've ever met. I may lose another friend too, you.

Perhaps you're thinking that all this mountain air has gone to my head. It has. Lucky me.

Phoebe

TWENTY-EIGHT

FATHER IS IN RIDGE all the time now. Mr. Spencer is here a lot too, not only to see Daisy, but also to help Father work on the dance floor. Daisy and I keep the house running smoothly. Paulie is mostly with Father and Mr. Spencer. We all take care of Mother. We all watch her closely. We all are afraid. There isn't any laughter any more. Joy has seeped out of our cabin like smoke from a chimney. In what is usually a sunny place, a cloud of sadness hangs over our cabin alone.

I miss Jed. It brings me to tears when I think my days with him, skipping stones, hanging from a rope and swinging over a pond, climbing trees, and hearing his laugh are over. He knows sadness. He'd understand how I'm feeling. It hurts to lose a friend like Jed.

Fall comes early to the mountains. Mornings are chilly

now, the air crisp. The outline of things is sharp, the line of the roof of our cabin set against the sky, the ribbon of Bear Creek looping through the canyon below, the wavy silhouette of the foothills beyond the lake, the intense greenness of the pines. Change is in the air. No one has mentioned school to me. I'm glad. As hard and sad as things are now, this is where I want and need to be.

I'm tired tonight. We ate dinner early. Dusk comes in the late afternoon now. Mother sleeps most of the time. I'm not in the mood to do much after we eat. I help Daisy with the chores and then lie on my bed and listen to Father, Paulie, and Mr. Spencer hammer away outside on the dance floor, wishing for sleep.

Outside the light is hazy, as if a thick cloud has sunk down and I am inside of it. I hear music, a waltz. From my loft window, strangely, I can see Father clearly. He is standing on the dance floor, completed now, dressed in his finest tuxedo, complete with tails and white gloves. Tall and confident, he extends an arm into the mist, palm open.

From the haze Mother walks toward Father. The scene is crystal clear. She's as beautiful and radiant as I've ever seen her. Her eyes sparkle and latch onto Father's. Nothing can come between them. Mother's cheeks are glowing with health. Her violet-blue, columbine-colored gown swishes and sways as they start to dance.

Sewn on top of each shoulder are flower petals that move as she dances. A line of stitched pearls spiraling down her dress is meant to show their windswept path. I am caught in the minutest of details, and yet I can also see everything at once.

My parents dance with their usual grace, and then something more, as if they know it is to be their last dance together until they meet again in heaven. They glide effortlessly, smooth and confident, around the dance floor built among the trees. Simple. Elegant. Breathtaking. Nothing less.

I am the only one watching them. On one twirl, Mother lifts her eyes to mine. Is she saying goodbye?

The music fades. Mother's feet are not on the dance floor any more. The mist is closing in around her. The edges of things blur. Father is all alone now and crying. I have to look away.

When I wake up, for the first time in my life, I do not want to get out of bed.

TWENTY-NINE

B UT I DO. IT is too quiet, too cold, and too sad. I've never taken these stairs so slowly. I'm afraid to get to the bottom. It feels like I am alone in this cabin, even though I know Paulie is still asleep upstairs in his bed. I've never come downstairs before so filled with dread and thinking that my world has changed for the worst.

When I reach the bottom of the stairs, I stop and take a breath. My legs are shaking, as if the floor beneath me is shifting. I have a choice. I can go into mother's room or the kitchen.

Usually Daisy is whipping up breakfast this time of morning. The kitchen is empty. It doesn't look like she's been in here since last night. I glance outside the window and am amazed how normal it seems, the sky its usual deep blue. There is a bluebird on a pine branch, chickadees flitting about. The sun is coming up. Light is filling the kitchen. How can this be? Outside is not any different from any other morning. Inside, my world is collapsing. I do not know whether Mother is alive or not.

There are footsteps outside, Daisy's. I recognize her brisk clomp-clomp. She comes into the kitchen carrying a bouquet of freshly picked flowers in her hand. When she sees my face, she gets down on her knees and opens her arms to me. I run into them. "Poor scared girl," she says.

She strokes my head with her hand. "These are for your mother. I'm late this morning. Was up most of the night with your father. We think she's turned a corner, that the worst is behind her. She's sleeping now, a good deep sleep, the first like that in a long while. She'll be hungry when she wakes up."

I pull back and look at her in disbelief, not quite knowing if she really has said those words or I have imagined them. "She's going to be okay, Phoebe."

We cry. We hug. And then Daisy is up on her feet, her usual self, all bustle, all business, and ever in a hurry. I help her whip up the batter and soon I have a plate of her full-moon pancakes in front of me. I get a warmed pitcher of maple syrup from the stove and pour it over them in swirly loops. Daisy rabbit-twitches her nose in the rising steam from the plate. We laugh.

I take the plate into Mother. Father is sitting with her on the side of the bed. Beaming with joy.

We are back in Denver now. School has started. Mother is taking things slow, but her health is rapidly improving. I get the sense she wants to make up for lost time. We all tell her to slow down, but she is undeterred.

She's gone to a meeting of the newly formed Audubon club in Denver. This doesn't surprise me. There are more teas scheduled. She has promised to take me to one.

Lisbeth knows now about how my mother and me feel about wearing bird feathers on a hat. She did come up to me at school though saying she had heard about my mother getting better and was glad. I believed her. Perhaps it was her way to of acknowledging my letter. Father did make the right decision for all of us, and especially Mother, by bringing her to Ridge and not, as Lisbeth would have had it, to a sanatorium in Denver.

I sense a growing distance between Lisbeth and me. It feels okay.

I think of the great blue heron a lot these days. I consider him my friend. My silence to Jed on the whereabouts of his nest is no guarantee that the heron's life will be spared. Jed may have found the nest on his own. Perhaps he already has. Or another hunter may have seen it.

But what I've done matters. As small as it is.

I want to do more.

There is a bright spot on the horizon. Daisy and Mr. Spencer are to be married in October in Ridge. They will live there and we will get to see them in the summer when we go to our cabin. I can't wait for their wedding. Daisy's joy at her future is making us all feel giddy. She cries because of not wanting to leave our family, and yet she still blushes when the conversation turns to Mr. Spencer. Her crying and then blushing make me laugh. And when I laugh, Paulie does too. We went without it for too long.

To my surprise, Father, Mother, and I are invited to Bonnie's wedding at the Brown Palace. We go. Mother and I wear jeweled hair clips. Father says we look radiant, glad we are not covered in feathers and bird parts. "Neither of you need that to look beautiful."

"Feathers belong on live birds, don't you think?" I ask.

"Yes," says Mother. "Nowhere else."

Every bit of the wedding planning, down to the last detail, makes the event a spectacle and we all get swept into it and have a good time. Bonnie looks beautiful. I think every bride must look that way on her wedding day. Lisbeth and I, when we are together, eat a lot of petit fours. We know the best ones to pick. Mother doesn't yet have the strength to dance, but she will. "By Daisy's wedding," she says.

Afterward, as the weeks pass at school, Lisbeth and I drift further apart. There doesn't seem to be any hard feelings between us. I study hard, work even harder in my drawing classes, birds mostly. My teachers and classmates like my work.

Time passes. I'm not afraid of Mother dying anymore.

THIRTY

I
T'S OCTOBER, AND WE took the early train to Morrisville. Now we are on the stage to Ridge for Daisy and Mr. Spencer's wedding. Mother wanted to sit up front with the driver, and so Father is in the backseat with Paulie and me. Mr. Spencer and Daisy will be married in a church. Father will give her away.

They've had some laughs over that. There was a time once, early on, when he would have liked nothing more. Now, he's sorry she's leaving us.

There will be a party after the ceremony at our cabin. Father's dance floor will be put to good use. Mother can't wait to dance. She's ready this time.

October is my favorite month. Golden-colored aspens brushstroke the mountainsides in color. It is a time of warm days and chilly nights. The cracks in the granite canyon walls carve lines that with little imagination turn into pictures of living creatures and other things. Bear Creek riffles along. I love its sound and take comfort in that it will always be there.

I remember our first trip to Ridge last summer. Father was so excited to tell me about our cabin. He put so much effort into making it the perfect place for Mother to get well. He never gave up hope, even when things got pretty bad.

Father looks at me with an expression that is odd to me. I am not sure what he is going to say next.

"Your friend, Jed, he really cared about Mother. Because he liked you."

So Father wants to talk about Jed. This surprises me. I wonder if Mother can hear us from the front seat. She must have told Father all about him. Funny thing, though, I don't think she ever met him. She didn't come to the bell ringing ceremony, where Father saw him. Didn't need to I guess. I told her everything.

I can't help but say the first thing that comes to my mind. "You called him a no-good lay-about. He's my friend."

Mother just accepted that any friend of mine was a friend of hers. Even if she never met him. But it wasn't that way with Father.

I quickly add, "Or was."

Father shakes his head. "I was wrong. I get too caught up in the shouldn'ts of this world. My daughter shouldn't climb trees, shouldn't befriend a local plume-hunter. No, Phoebe. You need to be you. I need to let you be you."

He pauses, confused. "Was? What do you mean *was* your friend?"

The words pour out of me, like a spring run-off, fast and without fear. I tell him about seeing the great blue heron, twice, and how he so moved me, and that Jed isn't my friend anymore because I refused to tell him the location of the nest. I've made his hard life ever harder.

"I'm sorry, Phoebe. You are a brave girl," Father says. Mother turns around. So she has been listening. I see it in her eyes that she knows how much it hurts to lose a friend. "I'm sorry, Phoebs."

There's nothing to say. Even Paulie is quiet, but it is a good silence.

"I suppose you could still tell him if you see him," Father says.

"I'm like you, not a go-backer," I say. "I will not change my mind, but Jed was my best friend at a time I needed a best friend. It's sad, that's all."

Father puts his hand to my cheek.

"Heron's View," I say. "What about that for the cabin's name. We never did decide."

Mother turns around again and says, "I think that's perfect."

It's as simple as that, naming a cabin, when the right name comes along. "Done," says Father.

Father spares nothing for Daisy's wedding. It is a simple service, none of the hullaballoo of Bonnie's wedding, but just as beautiful. More so I think. At the church Paulie and I tied ribbons onto That'll Do's bridle.

On the way to the party at our cabin, just as the procession of wagons and stages pass by the entrance to Mr. James's, Father gives the signal to his daughter who has been waiting for us there. She runs back into the bell grove and seconds later we hear the peal of bells. Loud. Every bell going full force.

Daisy is beside herself with joy. Nobody can talk while they are ringing. Goose pimples pop up on my arms. While I was ringing the bells over the summer, I know Father and I said prayers while we were doing it. Briefly I close my eyes again and pray a prayer of thanks. Father squeezes my hand. He must have done the same.

He can't know the pinch of sadness that is also in my heart. It's like when Mr. Spencer played his fiddle and gave us a sliver of joy when Mother was so sick. I guess it can work the other way too. On this most joyous of days, I am remembering ringing the bells with Jed, and wondering if I will ever see him again.

Father brought up an orchestra from Denver. The dance

floor is full of couples. Daisy has made sure the garden looks tended. The lavender, bell-flowers, and roses are still in bloom. "Live-forevers" she calls them. I think of my bird drawings. In a way those are "live-forevers" too.

Daisy had Father invite some of his and Mother's friends to the wedding. She thinks that after they see our cabin they will want Mr. Spencer to build them one too. It's a good idea, but Mr. Spencer is already a busy man. "A good problem to have," Daisy says.

Mother and Father dance, and dance, and dance. When Father is too tuckered to go on, he insists on their taking a break.

A lady is speaking to Mother. She looks familiar, but I can't place her. Mother introduces me to her. Apparently her husband works with Father. When she bends over slightly to shake my hand. I recognize the jeweled clip in her hair. She is one of the ladies who sat next to us at the Brown Palace that day I was there with Lisbeth to sample treats for Bonnie's wedding. She talked about what I now know to be Audubon Club of Denver. The one who smiled at me.

"I think what you are doing to try to protect birds is wonderful," I blurt out, and go on to tell her where I've seen her.

"It's a lot of work, but more and more people are joining the cause. We are trying to organize a tea for next month.

We have a woman from Boston coming to speak with us on how to get on firmer footing here in Denver. The Boston club is well established. I'm working on the invitations now, trying to find a good bird picture from a local artist to put on its cover."

"I want to come," I say, and then after her words sink in, add, "Wait!"

I run off to get my sketchbook. I have had the sense for a long time that the dance in my heart Miss Ruby uncovered is how I feel when I'm drawing. And now I'm getting the chance to open my heart further, to let some of the dance out, to share it with another person who may be able to use it for a greater good.

I show the lady my new drawing of a great blue heron, mid-flight, between the two big trees. "It's important to show birds in their natural homes," I say.

"Where they should be and remain for all times," says the lady. "It's perfect." She pauses, and then looks at my drawing again, and then at me.

"I wonder," she muses, and then asks the question that was already fluttering around inside of me. "May I use it for the invitations?"

I nod and stand straighter.

"And you'll get the first one in the mail soon," she adds, shaking my hand again.

Father takes me by the hand to the dance floor. He says he has the energy for just two more dances, one with Daisy, the other with me. I must have two left feet. Afterward he wants to know if he can give me dancing lessons in Denver.

I laugh. "I'd like that."

THIRTY-ONE

LATER THIS MORNING WE leave for Denver. We will not be in Ridge again until next summer. I'm taking one last walk down Bearberry Trail, both hoping to see Jed and not wanting to. I'm dressed in my city clothes. Those darn thorny buttons feel like a stick pressing against my back, and my fancy boots are no match for my favorite trail-walking ground grippers.

I've taken to the trail a few times in the last couple of days. Each time, when I don't see Jed, I am at once disappointed and relieved.

So of course today, just as I'm thinking about school, art classes, and the Audubon club teas in Denver, I hear Mike's bark. He bounds around the curve and runs right to me. I wrap my arms around him.

Jed's approach is slower, wary almost, as if he's unsure if

there's anything left of our friendship. He's carrying his rifle and an empty game bag. It's good to see him.

"Heard 'bout yur Ma," he says. "I'm glad things turned good for her."

He means that. I know it as sure as sure can be. He carries a big scar on his heart, the scar of his own mother dying, around which everything in his life has had to adjust.

I nod. "She likes you Jed, always did, from the start."

He scuffs the tow of his boot on the worn dirt trail.

"How have you been?" I ask.

The news comes sudden and hard.

"Pa says we're to be movin' on soon. Huntin' just aint' good here anymur."

The light is gone from his eyes. "Ya' saw one," he says, his voice almost a whisper. The force behind it though is as loud as a thunderclap at the summit of Mt. Veil. The wedge between us is growing wider by the second. I resist the urge to tell him want he wants to know, to bring my best friend back to me.

"Come on, Mike," he calls. "Bye Phoebe," he says, flatly.

He doesn't call me Phoebs, or Miss Fancy P's. They are almost out of sight when I shout, "Jed!"

He turns around to face me. I wonder if he thinks that I've changed my mind.

I do it quickly, before I lose my nerve, cartwheel, once,

my red petticoat flaring as I'm on my hands, first one and then the other. Then I wave.

He waves back. I can't say for sure, but I think he's smiling, as least a little bit. It means everything to me, that wave and a maybe smile.

"I'll miss you Jed," I say to the wind as Jed and Mike disappear from my life forever.

A tear runs down my cheek onto my lips. I taste its saltiness. "Live-forevers" surround me. Tall pines. Whispering aspens. A warm sun. Clear light. Rushing creek water down the canyon. Crisp, pine-scented air. And especially, birds and birdsong.

THE END

AUTHOR'S NOTE

THIS STORY WAS INSPIRED by Sarah Orne Jewett's classic short story, "A White Heron," published in 1886. Jewett was committed to the protection of birds in a time when it was fashionable for women to wear feathered millinery. Her story helped to awaken conservation causes that were just getting underway in the United States and which still resonate in the current environmental movement.

That same year, in 1886, poet Celia Thaxter wrote an essay called "Women's Heartlessness." In colorful language, she was the first writer to link the subjects of fashion and conservation. She describes a woman who, after laughing at a speech about protecting birds, walks away, "A charnel-house of beaks and claws and bones and feathers and glass eyes upon her fatuous head."

Both of these women were influential members of the

Audubon Society, whose mission in those early days was to save birds that were being hunted to the point of extinction. George Bird Grinnell founded the Audubon Society in the late 1800s in memory of John James Audubon (1787-1851), an explorer and artist whose admiration for birds inspired his famous paintings.

Fledging Audubon groups began forming across the country, often in the form of women's teas. In a time when women had little or no political voice, these gatherings gained strength and propelled the momentum for influencing change in the way people thought about killing birds for millinery purposes to the eventual legislation for their protection. People were drawn to Audubon Clubs in many ways. Phoebe Greer's story is just one of an untold number.

Today there are over 600,000 members of the National Audubon Society. Its mission has expanded worldwide to protect and restore at-risk bird species. In so doing the Audubon Society tackles current, relevant, and pressing environmental issues such as climatic threats and catastrophic oil spills. Their commitment to present-day issues ensures that their good work will continue for generations to come.

CPSIA information can be obtained
at www.ICGtesting.com
Printed in the USA
LVOW12s2317310518
579102LV00042B/52/P